Praise for Jaci Burton's *Dare to Love*

"If you enjoy an entertaining contemporary romance that is so full of heat that it may scorch you, this is definitely the book for you. Dare to Love is a fun, fast-paced romance full of love, life and everything in between."

~ *Jacquelyn, The Romance Studio*

"Jaci Burton is a fantastic storyteller and Dare to Love keeps you glued to your seat from the very beginning. I read this all in one sitting – I could not put it down...I am Joyfully Recommending Dare to Love and it is definitely one for the keeper shelf."

~ *Vivian, Joyfully Reviewed*

"Jaci Burton is one author you can always count on to write wonderful, sexy romances."

~ *Katie, Fallen Angel's Reviews*

Look for these titles by

Jaci Burton

Now Available:

Nothing Personal

Rescue Me

Show Me

Unwrapped

Unraveled

Print Anthology

Holiday Seduction

Dare to Love

Jaci Burton

A Samhain Publishing, Ltd. publication.

Samhain Publishing, Ltd.
577 Mulberry Street, Suite 1520
Macon, GA 31201
www.samhainpublishing.com

Print ISBN: 978-1-60504-279-4
Digital ISBN: 1-60504-081-9

Editing by Angela James
Cover by Scott Carpenter

First Samhain Publishing, Ltd. electronic publication: July 2008
First Samhain Publishing, Ltd. print publication: May 2009

Dedication

To all the ironworkers, the "cowboys of the sky" who risk their lives to construct the beautiful buildings rising high above the skyline, you have my admiration and my awe.

And especially to my husband, Charlie, who's one of them.

Chapter One

How could a man of the twenty-first century think he could arrange a marriage for his daughter? Was he insane? Then again, it was her father she was talking about, and Raymond Fairchild was in a league all his own.

"Certifiable, that's what he is. My father has completely lost it. Thinking he can marry me off like this is the freakin' eighteenth century or something." Lucy Fairchild stormed the sidewalk with her relentless pace, kicking at the rocks in her path. She knew she was talking to herself, but didn't care. Not that anyone could hear her with all the noisy construction going on.

She ignored the sounds of jackhammers and maneuvering cranes. Coupled with the daily mix of trolley cars and traffic forever permeating San Francisco's financial district, the sounds were just more white noise in an ever-busy city. Besides, her mind still whirled from the argument she'd just had with her father. Raymond Fairchild may be the president of one of the city's most prestigious law firms, but that didn't give him the right to control her life.

Right. Like that had ever stopped him from trying to control and otherwise lead her around as if she were too stupid to make her own decisions. She'd always gone along with him before. One, because he was her father and she loved him, and two, sometimes it was easier to do as he asked so he'd quit hounding her. Typically his machinations were harmless.

But marriage to a man of his choice? That's where she drew the line. The entire notion was positively medieval. She'd pick her own damn husband. Some day. When she was ready.

"Careful, darlin', you might trip and break one of those pretty legs."

She halted at the voice shouting at her, her ire rising by the second. Lifting her head, she spotted a group of men loitering near a construction trailer, smiling in her direction. This she did not need today.

"You lost, honey? I can help you find your way."

She should just walk past, ignore them. But their catcalling made her feel more like a piece of meat than her father's ludicrous statement that he'd just found the perfect husband for her.

Ignoring the clumps of dirt scuffing her black suede pumps, she stomped over to the group of five men, leveling her best courtroom glare.

"Do you know how insulting it is to be spoken to that way?"

One of the men, surely old enough to know better, grinned at her. "We're just bein' friendly."

"Those are not compliments." She shook her finger at his nose. His eyes widened and he backed up a step as she closed in on him. She heard the laughter of the other men, but ignored them. If necessary, she'd deal with them all, one at a time. "They're demeaning, harassing, and I have half a mind to report you to your boss."

"Report away. I'm right here."

She turned at the sound of the deep, resonant voice behind her and watched him stroll toward her. Obviously, the boss. Darn fine looking one, too. Mid-thirties, she'd guess, with dark hair that ruffled lightly in the late afternoon wind. His dusty jeans and work shirt couldn't hide the muscular physique that was most likely due to hours working on a construction site.

"Call off your dogs," Lucy said. For a moment, she'd been so mesmerized by the man heading toward her that she'd forgotten all about her irritation at the cavemen who worked for him. His smirk brought all her frustration back.

"They're just playing with you, having a little fun." He turned to the group still loitering and hooked a thumb at the gigantic steel structure across the street. "Break's over. Back to work."

With a great amount of laughter, elbow jabbing and mumbling, all obviously at her expense, they turned and headed toward the building.

A red haze of fury blinded her. "Can't you do something about your men? Every day I walk this way to get coffee, and every day they whistle and call out to me."

He shrugged. "They think you're good looking. Is that a crime? Believe me, they're harmless."

What a Neanderthal attitude. Were all men this dense? "Not to me they aren't."

He raised a dark brow and pulled off his sunglasses, giving her a knock-her-to-the-floor gander at his warm, whiskey-colored eyes. Eyes a woman could get lost in. She'd bet they'd probably turn a molten amber when filled with passion.

Okay, where had that come from? She tamped down the thought and focused on what he was saying.

"—and if you weren't so uptight about it, you'd just let it go."

"Excuse me? Uptight?"

"Yeah. Uptight. You know, like those pointy-toed shoes that I'll bet are pinching your feet right now. And that skinny skirt that's probably cutting off your breath. Want me to spell it out for you?"

She followed his gaze to her designer shoes that *were* squeezing her toes, and tried not to agree that the mid-calf skirt was a little more than uncomfortable. The man was beyond irritating. Coupled with her father's treatment of her, she'd just about had it. "Look. I don't have the time to stand here and argue with you. Just keep your animals on a leash in the future."

With a swift turn of her heel on the gravel, she made to leave, but her foot slipped on the rocks and she went crashing into his arms.

Nothing like hitting a rock-hard chest to knock the

breath out of a girl. At least she could focus on her breathing instead of the horrendous embarrassment flooding through her.

"You okay?" he asked, his minty breath ruffling the side of her hair.

"Yeah. I think so." What a klutz. He should be laughing at her right now. All full of righteous indignation the moment before she almost fell on her butt.

He still held her, much too close. And she was way too aware of how good it felt, which irritated her more than the catcalls from his crew. Then she made the mistake of making eye contact and saw the amusement crinkling the corner of his eyes.

"Are you sure?"

Even his tone spoke of laughter. At her expense.

She wrenched her arms away. "I'm fine."

He dropped his hands and jammed them into the pockets of his jeans. "You're welcome. Next time I'll let you fall on your ass."

"You're just like those heathens over there," she shot back, then instantly felt a stab of guilt. He *had* kept her from falling. She could have at least thanked him. Mortal embarrassment obviously outweighed politeness.

His eyes hardened, darkening to a rich, coffee color. "Wait just a damn minute. These guys might not be the refined upper crust that you associate with, but they're decent, hardworking men. Just because you don't have a sense of humor is no reason to look down your nose at them."

Lucy straightened the jacket of her suit and lifted her chin. “I’ve never looked down my nose at them. I just think it would be more appropriate if they kept their comments to themselves.”

He crossed his arms and leaned against the light pole. “Why? Can’t take a compliment?”

She sniffed. “I can take compliments just fine, thank you, when they’re positive as opposed to degrading.”

“I heard what they said. Nothing degrading about it. You’re just a snob.”

How dare he call her a snob? She was the least snobby person she knew, and she knew plenty of people who could easily be classified that way. His comment cut deep, because she’d always prided herself on trying to get to know people in all walks of life. Unlike her father and grandfather, who turned up their noses at anyone not in their small social circle. She found that type of elitist attitude appalling.

And she wasn’t like them. Not at all.

“I am not a snob. I just don’t appreciate being ogled and harassed while walking down the street.”

“First off, you weren’t being harassed. Second, yeah, you were being ogled, and why would that bother you?” Amusement colored his eyes back to that dreamy whiskey shade. “Not used to the attention? Understandable, considering your attitude.”

Why was she even having a conversation with this idiot? He was baiting her, she knew it, and still she stood her ground. If she had any sense at all she’d simply walk away.

But something about him got to her. “I get plenty of attention.”

He snorted. “Yeah right. From those uppity suit types who wouldn’t know what to do with a woman if she fell right into the middle of their balance sheets.”

Lucy resisted the urge to smile at that comment, knowing several men who fit that description. She’d even dated some of them. Boring as financial statements, too.

Instead, she decided to turn the tables. “And I suppose you know exactly what to do with a woman?”

Oh why couldn’t she learn to keep her mouth shut?

His full lips curled upward, transforming his tanned face into a work of art. A strong jaw sprinkled with a sexy dose of stubble lent him an outlaw look that made her pulse race faster. She felt the heat like a slap of lightning.

“Damn straight I know what to do with a woman. Would you like me to show you?”

She’d walked right into that one. Suddenly at a loss for words, her idiotic mind conjured up images of him doing just that. She shook her head, vehemently expressing her denial to both him and herself. “No, thanks.”

“Too bad.” He dug his well worn work boots into the dirt along the side of the road. “You’ll never know what you missed.”

“Doubtfully anything,” she lied, unable to believe she was still there. But something about him compelled her to stay. Maybe it was the pure enjoyment of sparring with someone who wasn't stuffy and boring. He had a generous wit and intelligence that belied his occupation. Plus he wasn't half bad to look at.

"You're not my type, anyway." His eyes twinkled with amusement in the afternoon sun. He was enjoying this.

This was her own fault. She'd stayed. Now it was a game of one-upmanship. And she hated to lose. "And, what, exactly, is your type?"

"Someone who wants to have fun. You're too straight-laced and tight a— Uh, uptight to enjoy anything but high tea or a rousing game of bridge."

She wrinkled her nose at the thought of having to endure either of those activities. He knew so little about her. "I'll have you know I am tons of fun." Yeah right. When was the last time she actually had a good time doing anything? She couldn't remember.

"Prove it. Go out with me."

Her heart thudded against her ribs before skidding to a complete halt. It took her a second to find her voice before she could say, "Excuse me?"

"Go out with me. Take a walk on the wild side. Or are you too afraid you'll get your perfectly manicured hands a little dirty?"

She looked down at hands that fit his exact description, then back up at him. For a brief second she had actually felt guilty because of who she was. "I'm not afraid of anything."

"Well?"

Great. She'd dug herself one incredible hole now. It would be easy to claim she'd been joking and merely walk away. She didn't even know the man's name, nor anything about him. Except the fact he was fine looking and had sent her hormones speeding in a direction they'd never been before.

"Umm..."

He nodded, wiping his hands on his jeans. "Thought so. See you around." He pivoted toward the nearby trailer.

"Wait!"

Oh God, had she just said that? He stopped and turned his head. Lord was he sexy, giving her that half-lidded gaze over his shoulder. And what incredible shoulders they were. Now that she'd opened her mouth, what was she going to do?

"Yeah?"

No, Lucy. Walk away. Do not do this. But that little niggling reminder of her father's excessive control over her life pushed her into doing something that was completely out of character for her.

"I'll go out with you." She waited for the feeling of dread to settle over her, but instead it felt right.

He tilted his head and smiled, then walked back to her and held out his hand. "Well, aren't you brave? Jake. Jake Dalton."

Jake. Now he had a name. She slid her hand in his and immediately felt the searing contact. His rough, callused palms scraped against her sensitive skin, sending shivers up her arm. "Lucy Fairchild."

"Okay, Lucy Fairchild, we'll have a date and see how it goes," he said with a charming grin.

Obviously he wasn't taking this any more seriously than she was. And besides, what was the harm? It wasn't like they were a love match or anything. It was just a date. Really, more like a challenge. A dare. Like playing chicken—see who flinched first.

She pulled out her business card, scribbled on the back and handed it to him.

He took the card and read both sides, his eyebrows lifting when he looked up. "Esquire, huh? You're a lawyer?"

She nodded, eager to get away from this man who made her think too much about what was lacking in her life. What she'd never experienced, but wanted to. "Yes. I really have to go. My home address is on the back of the card."

"Fine. I'll pick you up at eight."

She started to walk away, but his words stopped her. She pivoted.

"Eight?" She swallowed. "Tonight?"

"Yeah. Tonight. You busy?"

"Um, well, that is..." Good heavens. Tonight? She hadn't really thought about doing it so soon. Or really, at all.

"Yes or no?"

He was waiting for her to back down. Chicken. Flinch. No way. "Eight works for me."

"Fine," he nodded. "See you then. Dress casual. You do know what that is, don't you? No evening gowns? Leave the tiara at home?"

She tilted her head and sighed. "Yes. Casual. Whatever. Eight it is."

With as much dignity as she could dredge up, she walked down the street, shaking her head and muttering to herself again.

"A date. With a stranger, and an annoying one at that. I must be insane. This is all Father's fault. If he hadn't upset me with his ridiculous marriage idea, I'd have never stopped to confront those men. Which means I'd have never engaged in conversation with Jake, and wouldn't be having a date with him tonight."

She stopped at the coffee shop, her original destination after she'd stormed out of her father's office. She'd merely wanted a chance to cool off, to gain some perspective, and needed to get out of Fairchild's stuffy offices to grab a cup of coffee.

Then she'd run into those men. And Jake.

After ordering her latte, she took the steaming brew and sat at one of the small metal tables near the window, watching the red steel structure that would someday be a new high rise. Men worked on the upper levels of those skinny beams, walking the narrow steel structure with finesse and grace. She sipped her latte and watched for awhile, wondering if one of those figures up there was Jake.

Jake Dalton. Now there was expert construction.

She'd known many handsome men, men with athletic bodies owed to hours in the gym with a high-priced personal trainer. Men who went for weekly facials and had their hair cut by the best stylists San Francisco had to offer. They even got manicures and pedicures. All phony perfection that didn't do a thing to turn her on.

But never had she seen a man so well put together as Jake. His lean body was a result of hard hands-on labor, his tanned skin not from a booth with ultraviolet lights, but from hours spent working outside. His hair was unkempt and mussed, not perfectly combed and styled. The kind of hair that would be soft, that a woman would want to run her hands through and know that her fingers wouldn't get stuck in some kind of styling goo.

But he was utterly and completely wrong for her. They had nothing in common. He was more annoying than a summer fly in the house and she'd probably want to swat him by the end of their date tonight.

Unfortunately, she'd never been more attracted to a man in her entire thirty years of life.

Which was the precipitator of her father's conversation with her this morning that had set her off in the first place.

Her advancing age, as he'd informed her. The fact she wasn't getting any younger and hadn't once dated a man who was worthy of merging with the Fairchild family and producing an heir.

Merging. Like anyone she'd marry would be a business deal, not a love match. She'd like to show him a merger. Wouldn't he just have a fit when Jake Dalton showed up at the door tonight?

That alone would make the date worthwhile.

Though it wasn't really a date.

"I hear you got a date for tonight."

Jake cringed when he walked through the door of the construction trailer to find Bob Dixon grinning like he'd just won the lottery. The old man never failed to find ways to annoy him.

But without Bob, God only knows what would have happened to Jake. From day one Bob had been both his mentor and fiercest persecutor, ever since Jake had left home at sixteen and lied his way onto the construction crew Bob supervised.

Back then Jake had wondered if he'd even get hired on anywhere, and if not, how he'd manage the eating and roof over his head part.

All those years alone had made Jake resourceful. Bob had taken pity on the skinny kid with no skills and trained him. Bob Dixon had been more father to Jake than his own had ever been. So he put up with the old man's bizarre sense of humor.

"And they say women are gossips?" Jake threw his clipboard on the desk and faced the other man.

Bob laughed, a big belly laugh that fit his lumberjack-sized frame. "Men are bigger gossips than women, sometimes. So, tell me about her."

"Not much to tell."

Bob raised a bushy brow. "You liked her enough to ask her out."

"What? Am I wired for sound here?"

"Nah, the guys just listened in, and then, ya know how they talk."

"Unfortunately, yeah. I know how they talk." Their talking was what had gotten him involved with Miss High on the Hill in the first place. Just what he didn't need in his life right now.

His mind should have been on business—on this job which was so critical to his fledgling company. The high rise was his first huge project, and if they did well there'd be more business coming their way. Enough that Jake would have to expand and hire more people.

Which meant growth, and that's what he aimed for. Building his business was all he ever thought about. Usually, anyway. Except at the moment his mind was occupied by a petite wildcat in lamb's clothing.

"Heard she gave them a hard time," Bob said, spitting tobacco juice into a nearby cup.

Jake smiled and leaned back in the chair. "Yeah, she sure did. Took them on with no fear. I've never seen anything like it."

And they'd well deserved it. Idiots. Bunch of grown men leering at a beautiful woman, and then shouting at her like teenagers out for a joyride to pick up chicks.

Not that he'd behaved any better. He shook his head,

amazed at his own big mouth. Like he didn't have enough to worry about, he'd gone and asked the little tigress out on a date. He was way out of his league with that one. But her snobbish attitude got to him.

"Just the kind of woman you need. Somebody with a little fire, maybe light one under your too-long-a-bachelor rear end." Bob winked at him, the wrinkles around his eyes smiling.

"I don't need a woman at all." Women were complications that he didn't have time for. And he especially didn't need a woman like Lucy Fairchild. He'd spent his entire childhood listening to someone rail at him about not being good enough, about not measuring up.

His father's constant barrage of degrading comments still lived inside him, just waiting for failure to rear its ugly head and prove his father's words true. How he'd never amount to anything. How he was useless and stupid, and as worthless as his mother.

Even years later, despite building a successful business, those words stayed with him, haunted him. They hid inside him, not growing, but never going away. He'd spent all these years trying to prove his father wrong. He might be a blue collar worker, but he'd make a success of his life.

"Come on, Bob. You know how busy I am. The last thing I have time for is a woman."

"That's where you're wrong, boy." Bob lifted his heavy girth out of the chair, which creaked in relief at its offloaded burden. On the way past Jake's desk, he squeezed his shoulder. Jake looked up at him. “You’ve spent a lifetime runnin’ from that ghost of your daddy. You need to put that to rest. It’s time to find a good woman who’ll appreciate what you got to offer.”

Maybe Bob was right. Jake had spent all these years learning the trade, saving his money, working toward the day he could start his own business.

And when he had, he’d worked like the devil was chasing him trying to build it up. Now he was thirty-five years old, and if he was going to get married and have kids, he probably should get out there and find a woman.

But Lucy Fairchild certainly wasn’t going to be that woman.

“She’s not my type.”

Bob laughed and spit. “That’s what we all say. Right up until they lead us down the aisle.”

“She’s a rich career girl. You know I don’t date girls like that.” He’d never let anyone make him feel the way his father had. No, he stuck to his own kind. Girls who weren’t born into money, who wouldn’t look down on someone whose blood wasn’t blue like theirs.

“Hey, you’re the one who asked her for a date. I guess you’re stuck.”

True enough. Talk about a disaster. She’d probably expect some fancy, expensive restaurant that wasn’t in his budget. Too bad. She’d have to make do with the kind of place he liked to eat.

“Lemme ask you a question,” Bob said.

"Shoot."

"If this woman's such a snob, if she stands for everything you hate, why did you ask her to go out with you?"

"Hell if I know."

But he did know. After Bob left the trailer, Jake sat at his desk and propped his feet up.

He knew exactly why. Because she was gorgeous. The first thing he'd noticed were her long legs and curvy body. Then her wild, curly hair that flew everywhere around her face, the tawny strands glittering in the sunlight.

Plus, she was interested in him. He'd been with enough women to recognize when one was attracted to him. Her sea green eyes had studied him, held him, measuring, assessing.

Wanting.

He knew all about want. There were a lot of things he wanted in life. Some he'd managed to get. Some he hadn't gotten yet, and some he never would.

Not a betting man, he'd still lay a wager that he could get Lucy Fairchild. Maybe not permanently, but at least for a while. Which was all he had time or inclination for, anyway. Going out and having some fun with a woman was great. A woman who wanted anything more from him could look elsewhere. He didn't know what Lucy wanted. Probably nothing. She didn't even really want to go out with him in the first place, any more than he'd wanted to go out with her.

The fact she wore a painful vulnerability on her face

like some women wore hot red lipstick wasn't his problem. If he spotted something in her akin to the aching loneliness he occasionally acknowledged within himself, then tough. He wasn't her savior. As it was, he could barely save himself.

She represented nothing but a challenge. And he liked challenges.

So, he'd show up at her doorstep tonight and see what happened. Take the rich girl out and show her a slice of life she'd probably never seen before. If nothing else, the night should be interesting.

Chapter Two

Lucy glanced at the grandfather clock in the front hallway and wrung her hands, mentally reviewing the speech she'd planned to give Jake when he showed up.

She wasn't going out with him. Making that date with him today had been a huge mistake, and one she chalked up to a mind too preoccupied by her father's notion of marrying her off. She hadn't had her wits about her and stupidly agreed to a date she now had no intention of keeping.

It would be a waste of both their time. They had nothing in common, and she had too many other things on her mind to dally with a construction worker. No matter how sexy said construction worker was.

She tamped down butterflies that felt like the San Francisco 49ers defensive line ramming the wall of her stomach. How silly. As a courtroom lawyer, she had argued plenty of cases in front of a judge, jury and audience. The guys at the law firm referred to her as Fearless Fairchild.

So why was she nervous about giving the brush-off to one man? Why was she relentlessly pacing the front hall, scuffing her tennis shoes against the polished marble entryway? And why had she dressed this way, in a pair of dark jeans, a white pullover sweater and tennis shoes? This wasn't her usual clothing choice for a first date.

A date she had no intention of going on.

"Ridiculous," she muttered, then turned into the library and flopped into one of the burgundy leather chairs next to the fireplace. The scents of wood oil, old books and her father's cherry pipe always calmed her.

She lifted her feet and propped them on the matching ottoman, tapping her fingers against the well-cushioned arm of the chair. The library was one of her favorite rooms. Not only did it house all the classic books she'd loved to read as a child, but its dark, heavy paneling and scattering of comfortable chairs reminded her of her college literature department's main hall.

She'd spent hours in there, reading and doing homework, always feeling a sense of home in the room. Plus, she'd loved the discussions they'd held there. From Chaucer to Shakespeare to the poetry of Keats and Thomas, she'd inhaled the classics.

But she'd only minored in English. Her major had been pre-law, where she was, in her father's often repeated words, *destined to follow in her family's footsteps and continue the great works of her ancestors, the Fairchilds.*

Her father's lecture still rang in her ears after all these years. Duty. Family. Law.

At times like this Lucy wished her mother hadn't died

when she was only six. Sometimes she yearned to have someone she could talk girl things with. She certainly couldn't bring her personal problems to her father. She could only imagine the horrified look on her father's face should she ever ask him for dating advice.

She sighed. At least her turmoil over family and business had momentarily taken her mind off preparing her summary rejection of Jake Dalton.

The doorbell rang and her gaze shot to the mantle clock. She was impressed that he was actually on time. She rose, dreading the way she was going to hurt his feelings, but knowing it was a necessity.

Lucy rounded the corner and gasped. Wonderful. Her father had gotten to the door first and was currently engaged in conversation with Jake. Like she needed this complication. She could have sworn her father said he had a late meeting this evening. What an unexpected and unpleasant surprise.

"I'm certain you must have the wrong house." Raymond Fairchild stood stiffly at the door, no doubt mere seconds away from slamming it in Jake's face.

"Not the wrong house," Jake said. "Lucy wrote it on her card."

She peeked around the library doorway and spied Jake handing her business card to her father, a wicked smile on his face. Jake wore jeans—nice, dark clean ones—and a polo shirt that hugged his broad shoulders and showed off his biceps. She sucked in a breath and let it out again on a sigh. What an incredibly handsome man.

"I don't care where you say you got this card, young man. My daughter has a fiancé and she is not, I repeat, not, going out with you tonight, tomorrow, or ever."

In typical Raymond Fairchild fashion, her father made to shut the door on Jake. Lucy surged past her momentary frozen state.

"Wait!" She flew out of the library and slid across the slick tiles, coming to a stop next to her father.

Graceful, thy name is not Lucy Fairchild.

How embarrassing.

Raymond peered down at her over his glasses, his blue eyes sharp as ever despite the fact he was now sixty-four years old. His formerly dark hair had turned white, which just made him look more elegant and refined than he had when he was younger.

She'd loved and worshiped him for as long as she had memories. But right now he irritated the heck out of her.

"I do *not* have a fiancé, Father." She glared at him before turning her gaze to Jake. "I'm sorry, Jake. My father didn't know you were coming. Please, come in."

When her father didn't budge, she backed against him and gave him a slight nudge with her hip before opening the door wide for Jake to step in.

"Thanks." Jake swept a look from her father to her, then grinned.

Amused, was he? Well, she didn't find this entire, awkward situation humorous at all.

"Lucille, please explain."

Lucy set her shoulders back and inhaled sharply. "Nothing to explain, Father. I have a date."

Raymond raised a patrician brow and scanned Jake before frowning back at her. "A date."

"Yes."

"With him."

"Yes."

"No."

"Yes."

"I think not."

"I think so."

"Lucille."

"Father."

Jake's snort interrupted what easily could have been an hour-long war of very short sentences.

"You find something amusing?" her father asked Jake.

"Yeah. You two are funny as hell. You should take this show on the road."

Lucy hid the smirk that threatened to erupt. And despite the fact she'd had her reasons for canceling their date, her father's arrogant attitude toward Jake had her making an about turn in her decision.

"Let's go, Jake."

"Lucille, you are *not* going out with this man. I forbid it!"

She turned to her father, carefully controlling the

fierce anger that threatened to boil into a sure-to-be-regretted-later eruption. "You do not get to tell me what to do, whom to see, or how to live my life. I'm an adult and capable of making my own choices. Goodnight, Father."

She grabbed Jake's arm and literally hauled him out the front door.

Jake opened the door on what looked to be a new, cherry red Chevy truck. Even had the back seat with the extra doors. And, my, was it tall. He held out his hand while she stepped onto the side rail and hoisted herself up.

"Lucille?" Jake asked with a chuckle as he hopped in on the other side.

"Oh, shut up," she said, the adrenaline rush brought about by the argument with her father still zinging through her nerve endings.

He gunned the engine loud enough for her father to hear. It roared in her ears and vibrated her seat. Massive, powerful, the truck was like barely contained testosterone on wheels.

Which pretty much described Jake Dalton. He slipped the car into gear and peeled away from the curb, burning rubber in his wake. Lucy hid the smile that lifted the corners of her mouth as she spied her father's rigid stance at the front window.

"Fiancé, huh?" he asked.

"No. No fiancé."

"I guess we're lucky you got out of there when you did."

"Why?"

"You might have been grounded and we'd have had to cancel our date tonight."

"Very funny." She was not in the mood for laughs made at her expense, since she was mortified at her father's behavior, and Jake wasn't making it any easier. "Can we just drop it?"

"Why? Don't you think it's funny?"

"Not in the least." Now she wished she hadn't agreed to the date after all. It was clear he was going to tease her all evening.

"Lighten up, *Lucille*," he said, accentuating her name.

"My name is Lucy."

"Is it?"

"All right. It's Lucille."

"After?"

She turned to him with a frown. "After?"

"Yeah. Surely your parents wouldn't name you that on a whim."

Now he hated her name. Lovely. "What's wrong with Lucille?"

"Nothing. It's just not..."

"Not what?"

"I dunno. Doesn't seem to suit you, I guess."

"I was named after my grandmother."

"Ah. Figured it was something like that. But I like the name Lucy. It fits you."

"Fits? How?"

When they stopped at a red light, he reached out and grasped an escaping tendril of her uncontrollable hair, letting it slide slowly through his fingers. She shivered at the brush of his knuckles against her cheek. "Short and sassy. Like you."

"Oh." She studied him, looking for signs of some joke at her expense, but he only turned his eyes back to the road.

Wow, it was really warm in the truck now.

The radio played softly in the background. Country music. She stole glances at him, watching as he tapped his fingers in time to a song about lost love and broken hearts.

"Where are we going?" She noticed they'd headed over the Bay Bridge into the east bay.

"It's a surprise," he answered, not taking his eyes off the road.

"Um, am I dressed appropriately?"

He glanced at her briefly, his fingers tightening on the steering wheel. "You look fine."

Fine? What did that mean? Could there be a more nondescript word than *fine*? For all she knew that was manspeak for *hideous*. She leaned against the door and rubbed her forehead with her index finger, feeling the beginning strains of a headache. This whole night had been a disaster so far. She'd be glad when it was over.

They pulled into Robbie's Ribs, a one-frame building

that looked more like a farmhouse than a restaurant.

"You like ribs?" Jake asked as he opened her door.

"I don't know."

He tilted his head and expertly cocked one brow in question. "What do you mean you don't know?"

"I've never had ribs."

Jake shook his head. "Figures."

"What figures?"

"Nothing. Come on."

He grabbed her hand and started off. His hand was warm, his fingers entwined with hers. The simplest gesture and it probably meant nothing to him, but Lucy felt tingles all the way to her toes. His grip was firm and he walked very close to her, his shoulder brushing hers all the way inside.

He held the door open for her, put his hand on the small of her back to lead her inside.

He liked to touch her. She noticed that.

She liked it.

She didn't want to like it.

But she did.

Interesting choice of restaurant for a date. The place was packed. And loud. Unlike anything Lucy had ever experienced. Entire families ate here, at tables that looked like dark picnic benches. Out of little plastic baskets lined with paper. And they ate with their fingers.

It smelled both sweet and spicy. Warm, and full of laughter. A family restaurant.

She followed Jake to a cafeteria-style counter where they slid trays along, telling the person behind the glass what to scoop on their plates. Not knowing what to choose, she relied on Jake's suggestion and ended up with a huge pile of ribs, beans, coleslaw and bread. They grabbed one of the smaller picnic tables and sat.

Okay, now what? Ribs and barbecue sauce, which she was supposed to eat with her fingers. The white sweater she'd chosen was fast looking like a bad choice of attire.

"Are you going to stare at the food all night or are you going to eat it?"

She looked up at Jake. "Um, how?"

He grinned and shook his head. "Lost without twelve utensils on each side, aren't you, honey?"

"Smartass."

He laughed, clearly not at all insulted. "They're ribs. Pick them up and eat with your fingers."

"Seriously?"

"Yeah. Everyone gets messy. It's allowed."

He dug into his meal, sauce lined on the sides of his mouth, seemingly unaffected by her dilemma. She couldn't very well try to cut a centimeter-sized piece of meat off the bone, now could she? With as much decorum as she could manage, she picked up a rib and bit into it.

She bit back a moan. Dear God, it was delicious. The meat was tender and fell off the bone into her mouth. The tangy sauce tickled her taste buds with its sweet and spicy flavor, and she found herself devouring the meal.

She even licked her fingers. By the time she'd finished and wiped her hands, she looked up and found Jake watching her. Intently.

"What?" she asked, sliding her tongue across her lips in case some barbecue sauce had failed to be swept away by her napkin.

"Don't do that." His gaze never left her mouth.

"Don't do what?"

"Lick your lips like that."

She stopped in the middle of her frantic tongue swiping and looked around. The only person who had an eye on her was Jake. "Why not?"

"It turns me on," he said with a wicked grin.

In an instant her throat went dry and her toes curled in her tennis shoes. "It does?"

"Yeah. Don't you know what a woman licking her lips like that does to a man?"

"Um, no." To the best of her recollection, no man had ever told her she turned him on. Especially not during dinner.

"You want me to tell you what kind of image that conjures up in my mind?"

Did she ever. She had her own visuals going and wondered if hers would match his. "No."

Desire flamed hot in his eyes. "You sure?"

No, she wasn't. She was dying to know. "Yes, I'm sure."

"Too bad. You ready to go?"

Since she couldn't indulge her fantasy about licking lips and Jake in this crowded, family-style restaurant, she supposed she was ready to leave.

She had never enjoyed a meal so much in her life. No one paid attention to where her napkin sat in her lap, or for that matter if she even had a napkin there. No one raised an eyebrow at the occasional slurp of her soft drink, and no one told her to take her elbows off the table. In fact, she was fairly certain it was a requirement here.

She probably could have burped and not a single soul would have batted an eyelash. The thought was appalling, yet made her want to giggle.

All in all, the evening hadn't been as bad as she'd anticipated. Granted, they hadn't talked much, but at least she'd survived it. And she hadn't had to make up some lame excuse to cancel out on him. Now he'd take her home, and that would be that.

Except he didn't. They drove a few miles down the road and Jake pulled into a gravel parking lot. The only building was a shack emblazoned with the name Murphy's. A bar. A tiny little bar no bigger than a one room house.

She glanced at him and he smiled, turning off the ignition. "How about a beer?"

Beer. Now that was something she hadn't had much of in her life. "Okay."

There were only a handful of cars in the parking lot. Several neon signs blinked on and off in the window. Jake grasped the handle of the paint-scarred wooden door and held it open for her.

It was completely dark inside, with the exception of a few lights over the bar and single pool table in the middle of the room. A few men sat at the bar watching a baseball game on television, and another two men were playing pool. Everyone turned to look as they walked in.

She was the only woman in the place. And these guys looked like they hadn't seen a female in years.

"They won't bite," he whispered into her ear and propelled her forward with his hand on the small of her back. "Unless you ask them to."

She shivered, whether from that suggestion or the feel of his palm on her back she wasn't sure. Either way, she felt comforted by Jake's presence. He seemed like the kind of man who could handle himself in a place like this.

He led her to a table in the back of the small room and left to get them drinks. Lucy sat ramrod straight in the hard wooden chair, her hands clasped on the table. Strains of soft oldies music played from the jukebox, and apparently her appearance in the place wore off quickly, because the men ignored her.

Jake returned with two bottles of beer. She sipped the cool liquid, sighing at a long forgotten pleasure. She hadn't had a beer since college.

"Not quite the elegance you're used to, is it?" he asked, arching a brow.

Was this some kind of test? A challenge? She shrugged in response. "It's fine."

He laughed and she bristled, knowing he was having

some sort of fun at her expense. So she wasn't used to eating at barbecue joints and having drinks in a one-room bar. That didn't make her a snob.

"Are you having fun?" she asked.

"It's fine," he mimicked.

She let out a huff, knowing she should never have agreed to this date. It was obvious they had nothing in common. She glanced at the clock on the wall above the bar, counting down the minutes until Jake would take her home.

"Why did your dad tell me you had a fiancé?"

The question threw her off kilter, and she found herself unable to answer.

"That's okay, you don't have to talk about it. Your fiancé has nothing to worry about from me. I promise I won't touch you."

"I don't have a fiancé," she answered, twirling her finger over the condensation on the beer bottle. And what did he mean he wouldn't touch her? Was she repugnant? They had seemed to make a connection in the restaurant. She had felt sparks, just as she did at the construction site this morning. Had she been wrong?

"I see. Well, no I don't see, actually. He thinks you have a fiancé, but you don't?"

"I don't want to talk about it."

"Fine."

She looked up at the sound of his clipped tone. Oh, man was he beautiful. Not gorgeous in a male model kind of way. His nose was wide and a touch crooked, and he looked like he needed a shave. Wisps of dark hair fell over his forehead, making her want to sweep them back with her hand. He was rugged. All male. Loaded with testosterone. Not a pretty boy, not refined, not impeccably tailored. Just a fine looking man. A real man. The kind of man who could literally sweep a woman off her feet. The kind of man a woman would want to grab by the shirt and kiss. Hard.

She felt flutters of arousal at the thought of what she'd like to do with Jake.

Time to change the subject before her fantasies got out of hand.

"My father wants me to get married," she blurted, then immediately winced. Now why on earth had she said that?

"Why?" He took a long swallow of his beer and leaned back in the chair.

Oh, why not give him something else to make fun of? "He thinks I'm getting older and it's time I settle down."

He offered a wry smile. "You're hardly reaching retirement age. I think you've got a few good years left on the old biological clock, don't you?"

"I'd like to think so."

"Is that the only reason he wants you to get married?"

How much should she tell him? Jake was a stranger and had made it perfectly clear that he was no more interested in her than she was in him. Worse, he made fun of her at every turn. Dare she give him more ammunition?

"There's this man my father thinks would be a good asset for the firm."

"Asset?"

"Alexander Sheldon. CEO of one of the big law firms in the city. Divorced, multimillionaire, and possibly interested in merging our two companies."

"*Company* being your family's law firm."

She nodded.

"So you're being bartered."

"No!"

His eyes widened at her shouted denial. She sunk down a little bit in her chair, now having managed to once again capture the attention of the men in there. "It's not like that at all."

"Then tell me what it is like."

"You wouldn't understand."

His eyes narrowed. "Why wouldn't I understand? Think I'm too dumb to comprehend the subtle nuances of the rich?"

"Oh, no, that's not what I meant at all." Without thinking, she slipped her hand over his and squeezed. God, she was failing miserably at this date.

He flipped his hand over, twining his fingers with hers. Her stomach dropped to her feet and her heart began to pound. And yet she didn't pull her hand away. He was like a magnet, drawing her ever closer. She liked touching him, and she really liked when he touched her.

Did he feel it too? That spark, like a pleasurable jolt that fired you up on the inside? She suddenly found it hard to breathe.

"Why can't you just pick your own guy?"

Indeed, why couldn't she? "That's my intention."

"But your dad sees it otherwise."

She pulled her hand away. His touch distracted her, made it hard to think straight. "My father is an honorable man, a very good man."

"But still, he's trying to control your life. A life you should be able to make decisions for on your own."

"I can handle my father. When I find the right man, I'll marry." She just needed to keep repeating that same phrase to her father, over and over and over again, hoping that some day it might actually penetrate his stubborn skull.

"Why don't you just get a boyfriend, or a fiancé? Get your father off your back?"

If only it were that easy. Of course, actually dating would be a good start. Funny how she never seemed to make time for that. "I will. Some day."

And in the meantime, her father would continually shove Alex at her. She shuddered at the thought.

Like anyone she'd marry would be a business deal, not a love match. And then he had the nerve to suggest that she could do worse than marrying Alex.

"Tell me about this Alexander Sheldon guy," Jake said.

She smirked. “Alex is the most relentless, vicious lawyer in the city. He’s never lost a case and never lets anyone forget it. The man takes egotistical to a new level.”

“Mmm, sounds like a great guy.” Jake smiled and winked at her.

Lucy rolled her eyes. “Oh, right. According to my father, Alex is perfect. Wealthy, career minded and, of course, from a very reputable family.”

Her father hadn’t been amused at all when she made the suggestion that *he* marry Alex if he thought Alex was so darn perfect. Under no circumstances would she ever settle for less than complete and utter love. She didn’t even like Alex.

“Yeah, I could see how something like that is important to people like you.”

Lucy looked up and met his gaze. “What does that mean?”

“Blood ties, lineage and all that. Can’t be mixing with the lower class now, can we?”

She felt the sharp bite of his words, knew in some convoluted way he referred to himself.

“To some people, I suppose that’s important.”

“But it isn’t to you.”

She met his gaze head on. “Not in the least.”

Jake looked down and worked on tearing the label off his bottle of beer. Had she hurt his feelings? Damn if she could figure out how to act in this situation. What a nightmare. She longed for the comfort and safety of her house, where she could hide from all the ugly realities of social class and family expectations.

"What about you?" She desperately needed to change the subject. "Don't you have someone in your life?"

His face tightened for an instant. Lucy recognized the look that crossed his face. She'd seen it enough times when she looked in the mirror. That empty expression, the one that signaled *lonely*.

"I'm too busy to settle down."

She let out a small laugh. "Now you sound like me."

"But I don't have a father trying to marry me off, either."

She grimaced, hating that they'd gotten back on that subject.

There had to be some way to get her father to let loose of this ridiculous marriage idea. Otherwise, every event she attended she'd be hounded by Alex, and her father.

"Maybe I need to find someone to parade around, let Father think I'm involved," she mumbled to herself.

"Good idea."

"It would have to be someone he didn't know. Otherwise he could manipulate the situation." She drew figure eights in the condensation on the beer bottle.

"Got someone in mind?"

"Not really. He knows everyone I know."

"You could use me."

She snapped her gaze up at him. "Pardon?"

"Use me. To keep your dad from playing

matchmaker."

Had she missed a vital part of their conversation? What in the world was he talking about? "I don't understand."

"It's simple. You let your father think you're dating me, and he won't be able to throw this Alex guy at you anymore."

She took a quick gulp of her beer, hoping the cool liquid would melt the lump in her throat. "You want to date me?"

He laughed. "No. Just help you out. Appearances and all."

This whole night had been a surreal experience. Had she just stepped into some outer dimension? She had to get her mind around the thoughts swirling through her. Her father. Jake. Alex. It was all too much.

"Why would you want to do that?"

He grinned. "Maybe I want to annoy your father."

Okay that made perfect sense. Her father had been anything but gracious to Jake. She still burned at his condescending manner.

The thought had merit. It was ludicrous of course, but still, parts of it intrigued her. How long had she fought against her father? Against his ridiculous notions of society and classes? How many times had he tried to drum into her head that the Fairchilds were the elite? The elite who did not, under any circumstances, mix with the lower classes.

Yes, her father was a snob. She'd spent her entire life trying not to emulate his actions. He would positively have a fit if she started parading Jake around as her boyfriend.

"Are you certain you'd want to do this?" Her mind spun with ideas.

"Why not? Might be fun to get a few digs into your old man."

She didn't really understand Jake's motivation in all this, but if she brought him to a few events and let her father know she wasn't going to be bought and sold like a piece of property, maybe he'd back off and let her make her own decisions. It wasn't like she and Jake would really be dating.

"I'd ask you to attend some social events with me. Just enough to let my father, and Alex, see us together."

"Whatever. As long as it doesn't interfere with my work."

"My father will not be pleasant about this, Jake. He can be rude, downright nasty at times."

Jake shrugged. "I've heard worse. Doesn't bother me a bit."

"We wouldn't be actually dating."

He nodded. "Right. Not dating."

"It might work. And it probably wouldn't take long. Once my father sees me with you a few times, he'll know I'm not interested in Alex, and maybe he'll drop all thoughts of trying to marry me off."

"No problem. And besides, after being with me, anyone you pick after that will be a huge relief to your father."

That thought hadn't occurred to her. Sadly, he was right. But how did Jake feel about that? His expression was unreadable. She didn't know if he was amused or annoyed, but either way, she was grateful for his help. She had to take control of her life, make her father understand that *she* would choose the man she would marry. Not that Jake was that man. But her father didn't need to know that.

Guilt niggled its way into her heart. This could be rough on Jake. Really rough. People in her circle looked down their noses at those who weren't born with the proverbial silver spoon in their mouths.

"Jake, I don't know. I'd feel awful if someone hurt your feelings."

He laughed. "Believe me, no one could hurt my feelings. I'm immune."

She didn't know how someone could become immune to being insulted. "What's in this for you?"

He shrugged. "Other than irritating your father, nothing. I need to get out more, anyway."

Somehow she didn't think he really meant that. "I'll bet you have a lot of dates."

He laughed. "I have a few now and then."

She shouldn't do this. She really shouldn't. But the more she thought about it, the more it seemed like the key to her freedom. Her father was a smart man. Surely he'd see right away that she wouldn't allow him to choose her husband.

"I can't believe you're doing this for me, but I appreciate it. And I'll try not to take up too much of your time."

He shrugged. "Whatever gets you off the hook, sweetheart. I'm glad to help out. And if it irks your old man in the process, all the better."

Okay, this was starting to sound like fun. And spending time with Jake wouldn't be a hardship at all. He was great looking, had a good sense of humor, he was smart, and, admittedly, she liked him. She really liked him. He made her feel good. She liked touching him.

"Let's dance."

She snapped her gaze to his. "What?"

She barely heard the music playing in the background. Jake stood and held out his hand. "Dance. Practice being together for when your dad sees us. You might as well get used to it now."

"Okay."

She stood and let Jake lead her to the...well, there really wasn't a dance floor in the place. Jake took a few steps away from the table and drew her against him.

Solid, warm, he wrapped his arm around her back and entwined his fingers with hers, then swayed to the music of a ballad.

"You're stiff as a board, Lucy. Your father will never believe we're dating if you don't loosen up."

He was right. She hadn't been ready for this. She really did need the practice.

"Look at me."

She tilted her head back and was instantly lost in the warm depth of his eyes. They held a sensual promise she'd love to explore, if only they had a real relationship.

So she'd pretend it was real. She could do that, couldn't she? She'd fantasize that Jake really did care about her, that he really was interested, that the spark of attraction she felt for him was returned.

The way he looked at her, the way his lips curled in such a sexy manner, the way he leaned in as if he was going to—

His lips brushed hers, casual, a soft caress. Lightning struck and she was rooted to the spot, unable to take her next breath. Then he pressed more firmly. Shocked at first, Lucy did nothing but freeze up.

Jake leaned back. "Don't tell me this is your first kiss."

"No. Of course not. I just...I didn't know you were going to kiss me."

He arched a brow. "Was I supposed to ask for permission?"

Her heart pounded, her hand began to sweat in his. Really, no wonder he thought her inexperienced. What an idiot. "I can do better."

"I'll just bet you can."

Could all men lower their voices and whisper in a way

that made a woman melt, or was it just Jake? She shivered as he leaned in again, and this time she was ready.

Or she thought she was ready, but not for the power of a kiss that rocked her right off her feet.

She'd expected more of the same, a light sweep of his lips against hers, a chaste, get-to-know-you kind of kiss.

Instead, he leaned her back over his arm and took her mouth in a kiss that spoke of possession, of demand, forcing her mouth open to slide his tongue inside.

Every part of her body exploded with sensation, with desire, with a hunger that hadn't been satisfied in far too long. She felt every part of that kiss in every nerve ending of her body.

When Jake raised her up and pulled away, she was dizzy, turned on and ready for more.

"Now when we're together in front of your dad, we'll act more like a couple," he said, taking her hand and leading her back to the table.

Disoriented, Lucy grabbed her beer and took a couple deep swallows.

Jake nursed his beer and grinned at her, seemingly unaffected by what had just happened.

He sure could turn it on and off easily, couldn't he?

But could she? Because she was hot and bothered as hell, and not at all ready to stop what he'd just started.

This game she'd agreed to might be more than she could handle.

A lot more.

Chapter Three

Jake was out of his mind. Certifiable. What had he been thinking, suggesting that Lucy use him to get her father off her back?

He couldn't even blame booze as the cause of his idiotic suggestion. He'd only had one beer when he made the offer to Lucy.

He could think of a lot of fun ways that Lucy Fairchild could use him. But as a boy toy? No thanks.

And kissing her? Yeah, that had been a huge mistake, because she'd tasted like everything he wanted, and knew he'd never be able to have. He was in way over his head on this one.

Shoving the paperwork on his desk aside, he grabbed his now cold coffee and headed to the counter for a warm up. How in hell was he going to get out of this mess he'd volunteered for? He had no time for this. Work was intensifying, he had bids to catch up on before he missed the deadlines, and he needed to be here every day to oversee the construction.

Spending time escorting Lucy around would be a colossal waste of his time. He had no relationship with her, had no interest in her other than their one date that was more a dare than anything. Though he couldn't say he wasn't attracted to her.

That wild, curly hair was like a part of her personality. A part she kept well hidden, if she even knew it existed. He'd love to be the one to unleash the fire he suspected she held deep inside. He'd bet a year's income that under that cool, socialite exterior beat the heart of a tigress. He'd sampled a bit of that wildness last night. It only left him craving more.

She was so damn vulnerable it made him ache. She'd looked lost sitting at the bar last night, mumbling about how to extricate herself from her father's clutches. The old man had her on a leash, trying to dictate how she should live her life.

And his little tigress didn't like it one bit. He could tell she was literally chomping at the bit to be free, but her father had some kind of hold on her, and she couldn't figure out how to get loose.

Yet. With a little help, she could. But dammit, why had he volunteered to be her rescuer?

"Uh oh. What's wrong?"

Jake turned at the sound of Bob's voice. "Just busy."

Bob climbed up the stairs and threw his clipboard on the desk. "You're scowling like you're pissed as hell about something."

Yeah, at himself. "Nah, nothing's wrong. Just trying to get my head around this project."

"You're doin' fine, kid. Don't worry about it. You got

the smarts that most people with them fancy degrees only wished they had. And you're a damn fine construction boss. Don't sweat it."

"Thanks." Easier said than done. He had to sweat it, had to worry about it. About everything. He couldn't fail.

"So, are you gonna tell me or will I have to pry it out of you like a dentist after tooth decay?"

"Tell you what?"

"About the date last night."

"Nothing much to tell." Maybe if he played it off like no big deal, Bob would let it drop.

"That good, huh?"

No such luck. "It was...interesting."

"How so?"

The man was worse than having a mother around. "Just interesting."

"You gonna see her again?"

"Not a chance," he lied. The last thing he needed right now was browbeating from Bob. The less he knew the better.

"Why not?"

Jake shrugged. "She's not my type."

Bob smirked, his devilish eyes full of glee. Jake didn't even want to think about what was rolling around the old man's head.

"Why isn't she your type?"

God, would the inquisition never end? "She's too

short, too big in the hips. She's conceited, talks all about herself, boring as hell and I'd rather spend a night at a bridge club tournament than have to put up with Lucy Fairchild again."

Bob spit his tobacco into the cup on the floor, then grinned like a madman. "She's standing right behind you."

Huh? He turned quickly to find the subject of their discussion standing at the entrance to the trailer, her arms folded across her chest, an annoyed look on her gorgeous face.

Oh, hell. How much had she heard?

"Was I mistaken last night when you mentioned you wanted to go out again? Because it sure sounded like you'd rather have brain surgery without anesthesia than another date with me."

Crap. She'd heard it all.

"I, uh, I, uh..."

"I wouldn't worry about that stuff he said, honey." Bob grinned at Lucy on his way out and said, "He just made up a pack of lies so I wouldn't make him admit how much he really does like you."

Lucy smiled at Bob and leveled a smirk in Jake's direction. "I'll keep his tendency to lie in mind. By the way, I'm Lucy Fairchild."

"Bob Dixon." Bob shook Lucy's hand, then made his escape.

Oh sure, Jake thought. Desert the captain of the ship

as he's about to be boarded by a ruthless pirate. A very irritated one at that.

"Sorry," he said as she stepped into the room. "Foot in mouth disease. I get it a lot."

"I meant what I said," she said, looking not at all comfortable standing in the middle of the room.

"Relax and sit down." He pulled a chair for her in front of his desk. "It's a little cramped in here, but you don't need to hover in the middle of the room."

"I'm fine standing."

Yeah, right. She looked about ready to sprint out the door. He wanted her to stay so he could look at her for a few minutes. She wore a business suit, same as yesterday, except this one was a green color that made her eyes stand out and grab his attention. And it wasn't quite as long as that calf length one she wore yesterday. This one hit her at the knee. Damn she had nice legs.

"Sit," he commanded, then winced. "Please."

Breathing out a sigh, she took the two steps necessary to reach his desk and sat at the edge of the chair, her back stiff and her chin lifted.

"I didn't mean anything I said to Bob, so wipe that stern lawyer look off your face. I told him I wasn't going to see you again because I don't need him bugging me with questions every time we go out."

She looked down at her skirt, wiping away imaginary crumbs or wrinkles or something. Whatever it was, she didn't want to look at him. "It was a stupid idea, anyway."

No it wasn't. "I don't think it's stupid."

Her eyes met his, her expression shouting her vulnerability. "You don't?"

He smiled. "No, I don't. Besides, we made a deal. I'm your date for however long you want to use me."

"I wish you wouldn't put it that way," she said, wrinkling her nose. "It sounds like I'm, well, like I'm using you."

"Aren't you?"

"No. Yes. Oh, I don't know." She stood, knocking her purse to the floor. He bent down and picked it up, taking just a second to admire the sexy curve of her calf. Resisting the urge to run his hands along those fine legs, he forced his fingers to grasp her purse, instead, then stood and handed it to her.

"Thanks."

Instead of backing away like he should, he stood where he was, mere inches from her.

She smelled good. Like fresh fruit in the summer. Sharp, tangy, citrusy. He wanted to lick that spot on her neck revealed when she turned her head to the side, see if she tasted as good as she smelled. He wanted to kiss her again like he had last night, only this time he didn't want to stop.

"I don't mind being used." He couldn't believe he was having this conversation with Lucy in his work trailer in the middle of the day. Anyone could walk in and find him all but panting and drooling over her. Wouldn't that give the guys a lot to talk about during lunch?

But damn if he could help the way she made him feel. He picked up one of those crazy curls that never seemed to want to stay put in that clip behind her head, slid his fingers over it, straightened it out as far as it would go, then let loose and watched it spring back into place. Her hair felt like soft butter.

"I should go," she said in a near breathless voice.

He'd like to get her to pant like that from something else, feel her chest rise and fall against his as she gasped for breath underneath him.

Damn. He shifted, hoping she wouldn't notice his growing interest in her.

"Should you?" He didn't want her to go. He wanted her to stand there the rest of the day and let him look at her, inhale her sweet fragrance, and think about what it would be like to touch her. Was her skin as soft as her hair? Would it mold against his hand like that curl did?

"Oh. I almost forgot why I came here." She took a quick step back, putting some distance between them. Jake shook his head to clear his mind.

"What is it?"

"There's a charity gala on Friday night. I was wondering if you'd go with me."

"Sure. What's the charity?"

"The Fairchild Foundation. We provide scholarships for underprivileged children."

"Impressive. Just tell me where and when."

"I'll pick you up in the limo."

He snorted a laugh. "I don't think so. Besides, I have a meeting in San Jose on Friday and I don't know when I'll get back. Best if I just meet you there."

She chewed her lower lip and then nodded. "All right. I'll give you the address. Oh, and you'll need a tux. I'll pay for it, of course."

"I can rent my own tux, and pay for it myself."

"No, really, I—"

"Lucy. I'll take care of it. I'm not a pauper, you know."

Her face was cute when she blushed, her cheeks turning all pink. "I'm sorry, I didn't mean to imply otherwise."

"No sweat."

She scribbled down the particulars and handed him the paper. "Friday night. Eight o'clock at the Hotel San Marcos on Van Ness."

"Okay. I'll see you there."

"I'll leave your name at the door."

"No problem."

"I'll let you get back to work now."

"See you later."

"Bye." With a last glance and quick smile over her shoulder, she stepped out of the trailer.

Jake exhaled. For such a simple discussion it had sure been intense. It was like both of them couldn't wait to get away from the other. Or maybe both of them couldn't wait to get closer.

Lucy did something to his libido, something he

normally had well under control. Typically he called the shots with women, but ever since he met Lucy Fairchild he was lucky to remember his own name let alone think about maintaining the upper hand.

He had to remember this was nothing but a game. And a short-lived one at that.

Besides, he had way too much work to do to be mooning over a woman. He couldn't afford to slip up now, not when he was so close to success that would banish the demons that had hounded him all these years.

Lucy paced outside the ballroom and checked her watch. It was ten minutes after eight. Not that most of the crowd wouldn't show up fashionably late, but she hoped Jake would just show up. She smoothed her hands over her hair, hoping by sheer force of will to keep the curls from springing free from her updo tonight. She had no time to battle a hair crisis.

She stopped to check her reflection in the lobby mirror. Hair still glued to her head in one piece, check. Off-the-shoulder, black velvet ball gown not revealing too much cleavage, check. Lipstick not stuck to her teeth, check.

Where was he? She checked her watch again, then palmed her somersaulting stomach. This was worse than the other day in the construction trailer with Jake.

She'd felt like a schoolgirl then, stumbling over her words and practically her own feet. How could a man covered in dust and grime, wearing stained jeans and a Dalton Construction T-shirt look so darn sexy? And how come she noticed that? She barely paid any attention to the designer-clad professionals at the firm. Something about Jake captured her interest, and held it.

But did she have to act like a tongue-tied teenager around him? Really, she was an adult and had plenty of dating experience, even a couple affairs, short lived though they were. It wasn't like she was inexperienced. Jake sure made her feel that way, though. Maybe it was the way he looked at her. Intense, giving her his full attention. She shivered at the way his gaze raked over her whenever they were in close proximity.

"You look lovely this evening."

Lucy turned hopefully in the direction of the male voice, hoping it was Jake. Her heart fell to her feet. Alex Sheldon. The last person on earth she wanted to be cornered by tonight. Or ever.

"Alex," she said coolly. As usual, not a hair out of place. Impeccably dressed, not even a lint speck. His sandy-colored hair was more glued together by goop than hers was. And his way-too-fake tan made his blue eyes look more icy than usual.

Immediate visions of dark hair and warm, whiskey eyes entered her thoughts. When she looked at Alex, she felt chilled to the bone.

"I see you came alone. How convenient, since I'm solo tonight, too." His smile was not at all genuine. The way he leered at her made her wish she'd brought a wrap to cover herself. The man gave her the shivers and not in a good way. Not in the same way Jake did.

"Actually, I'm expecting someone," she said, turning her head to focus on the brass etched lobby doors, hoping Alex would find someone else to annoy. "My date."

"Your father and I had a very productive meeting this morning."

"How nice." Obviously, he chose to ignore her blatant brush off. And in what alternate universe would she care about his meeting with her father?

"We discussed some things that were, shall I say, personal in nature?"

That got her attention and she turned to him. "Personal, how?"

He adjusted the cuffs of his tux and brushed imaginary lint from his sleeves. "Personal as it relates to you and me."

Oh, Lord, this couldn't be good. What had her father done now? "Just spell it out for me, Alex." She wasn't in the mood to play twenty questions with him.

"Your father intimated that you and I were very well suited. And I must say, I couldn't agree more."

He tilted his head toward her and winked. He actually, honest to God winked at her. She resisted the urge to gag. "I'm sorry to tell you that's only my father's opinion."

"Now, Lucille, you could do much worse than connecting with someone like me. If I do say so myself, I am considered quite a catch."

She'd like to toss him back out there for someone else to reel in. "Sorry, Alex. Not interested."

"I think with a little persuasion, you could be." He leaned in and ran his knuckles over her cheek. He reeked of wine, and it was only eight-thirty.

Okay, enough fun and games. She opened her mouth to tell him exactly what she thought of being negotiated like a commodity when a deep voice spoke behind her.

"Hey, pal, that's my woman you have your hands on."

Alex's hand froze and he turned a frigid gaze just over Lucy's left shoulder. Lucy's pulse kicked up a few notches when a warm hand slipped around her waist, turning her around to face her date for the evening.

Okay, this bordered on the ridiculous. She'd spent her entire life around men wearing tuxedos, and never had one taken her breath away like Jake did. He was magnificent. The tux was perfectly tailored for him, the jacket cut tight across his broad shoulders, the pants tapering in to fit snugly against his lean waist. The starched, white shirt provided a sharp contrast against his tanned neck. Perfect. Simple yet elegant, like the wearer.

"You clean up well," she said with a tentative smile, her heart hammering against her chest.

"And you're gorgeous." His gaze traveled the length of her.

Before she could utter her thanks, he pulled her against his chest, swept one hand along her neck, and pressed his lips firmly against hers in a kiss that would have knocked her socks off, had she been wearing any.

All sense of time and place was lost as Jake's mouth moved against hers, teasing her lips with the barest of pressure. She slid her hands into his hair and leaned into him, delighted in the feel of his fingers flexing against her waist.

His scent wafted over her. Not that chokingly expensive cologne that most men reeked of, but more like soap. Fresh, clean, and masculine in every sense of the word.

Her body fit his perfectly. She could stay in his arms forever, never needing another thing.

Oh, wow, she really liked kissing him.

A cough brought her back to reality. Jake pulled his lips from hers, his eyes dark, his breathing as labored as her own. "Sorry I'm late," he said with the hint of a smile.

Late? Late for what? It took her a few seconds to gather her bearings. Then Alex coughed again.

"It's all right," she replied in a voice too throaty to be her own. "You're worth waiting for."

"Who's your friend?" Jake's eyes narrowed.

Reluctantly, she turned to face Alex. "Jake Dalton, this is Alexander Sheldon."

Alex cocked a pale brow and put on his best patrician air as he briefly shook Jake's hand. "Dalton."

"Sheldon," Jake mimicked, looking none too pleased himself by the introduction.

"Any relation to the Daltons of New Hampshire?" Alex asked.

"Not that I'm aware of. My family's from the west coast."

"Ah, I see." Alex tapped an index finger against his pursed lips. "New money, then."

Jake laughed. "Any money I make is new to me."

She had to separate these two before an explosion occurred. She smiled sweetly at Jake. "I'm starving. Let's go inside and find our seats."

Jake held out his arm and Lucy slipped hers through. "Later, Sheldon," he said.

"I'll be counting on it," she heard Alex reply before she dragged Jake into the ballroom.

Jake couldn't hide his proud smile as they walked through the double doors into the ballroom. He never lost the thrill of seeing the finished product of what he'd started. Ten years ago he'd worked on this hotel. He remembered the intricate sloping roof that caused him and his crew fits.

"Why are you smiling?" Lucy asked.

"Just remembering the construction. I helped build this hotel."

Her eyes widened. "You did? It's a marvelous piece of architecture."

"It was a pain in the butt to weld the steel together."

"Really?"

"Yeah. What the architects put on paper and the ease

with which it transfers to steel erection are often like oil and water."

"I hadn't thought about that. But it truly is lovely, Jake. You should be proud to have been a part of it."

He was. Everything that carried part of his work he looked on with pride. He'd worked damn hard to get where he was, to learn what he'd learned through the years.

Jake allowed Lucy to lead him through a throng of people, most of whom she knew and waved at or stopped to greet. Which was fine with him since it gave him the chance to ogle her without her knowing.

Damn, she looked incredible. And way out of his league in the minors versus majors way. The black velvet dress dipped dangerously off her shoulders. Her full breasts swelled over the low-cut V-shape in the top, and every time she inhaled they threatened to spill over. He wondered how long it would take him to whip off his tux jacket and throw it over her in case her breasts accidentally fell out the top of the gown.

She wore no jewelry other than little pearls in her ears. But she didn't need any. The dress and the body in it were enough.

They reached a table at the front of the room, and Lucy directed him to his assigned seat next to her. It didn't take long for her father to come bearing down on them.

"What is *he* doing here?" he whispered.

Lucy heaved a breath. Jake tried to keep one eye on

her father and the other on her breasts.

"Father, we're in public and if you make a scene you will look ridiculous. Smile and pretend to be polite."

Raymond opened his mouth to speak, glared at his daughter, then stiffly inclined his head toward Jake. "Mr. Dalton."

"Mr. Fairchild." No way would Jake do anything to embarrass Lucy tonight. He smiled politely.

They had a relatively quiet and peaceful dinner, despite the fact Raymond invited Alex Sheldon to sit at their table. On the other side of Lucy, of course. Jake did his best to ignore the man, who seemed more focused on getting Lucy's attention. Fortunately, Lucy's attention stayed on Jake.

A fact he didn't mind one bit. They made small talk and she asked him about his work, he asked about hers, but they never got into any serious discussion since both Raymond and Alex eavesdropped on every word they spoke.

"So, you're in construction." Alex said the word as if Jake sifted through people's trash for a living.

"Jake helped build this hotel," Lucy said.

Jake noticed the way her eyes sparkled with pride. He liked that.

"Tell me," Alex said, lifting yet another glass of wine to his lips. "Which style of Victorian homes so indicative of San Francisco architecture are your favorite? I tend to prefer the Italianate."

Before Jake could respond, Lucy stood. “Let’s dance,” she said, holding out her hand.

Despite his wanting to stuff Alex Sheldon’s superior tongue down his own throat, he nodded. How could he resist an offer of a dance with Lucy? They stepped onto the dance floor, the orchestra playing soft strains of an old melody that Jake couldn’t quite place.

She glided into his arms, her hip resting against his thigh. His palm splayed over the bare skin of her back. Silken soft skin, and that smell of summer.

“You really can dance.” Lucy lifted her head and met his gaze, surprise showing in her eyes.

“Thought I could only do the hoe down, did you? I didn’t get to show you my best stuff the other night at the bar.”

She laughed, and he found that he loved the sound. Deep and throaty, as if she could really belt out a good bit of giggling if she chose.

The music barely registering in his mind, he focused on Lucy’s cheek against his jaw, her full skirt billowing around his legs, the perfect feel of her in his arms. He tightened his hold on her and whirled her a few turns around the dance floor.

“I’m sorry about my father and Alex.”

He shrugged. “Don’t worry about it. I can take care of myself. Besides, isn’t that why I’m here?”

She tilted her head. “I suppose so.”

He’d give a million dollars just to kiss her neck.

Probably not a good idea to do that here.

"Still, it irritates me when they act so condescending and disapproving."

He slid his hand along the soft skin between her shoulder blades, enjoying her quick intake of breath. "I told you. Don't worry about me. I can handle whatever they throw my way."

She pulled in her lower lip and worried it with her teeth. His gaze was riveted on the short glimpse of her pink tongue, still tasting their kiss on his lips. What he wouldn't give to take a little nibble of that lip himself.

Unfortunately, the music ended. Lucy's face was flushed, her cheeks a rosy pink.

"You really *can* dance."

He smiled. "Had to take lame dancing lessons at school. I have a fairly good memory." He'd hated those classes when he was an early teen. Now he was grateful he'd had them.

They stood in the middle of the dance floor, neither of them moving. If he were a betting man, he'd lay a wager that Lucy Fairchild wanted another kiss.

Right here, in the middle of the dance floor, in front of all these rich socialites.

Wouldn't that cause a scandal? Jake thought it would be more than worth it to taste her sweet lips again.

"Please, excuse me for a moment." Her near breathless whisper told him she'd been thinking the same thing.

As soon as Lucy took off for the ladies room, Alex and Raymond approached him. Jake smiled behind his drink. They'd waited for the perfect opening like a couple of circling sharks scoping out prey. Now that they had him alone, he expected the inquisition. An inquisition he more than welcomed.

The night was about to get even more interesting.

Chapter Four

Lucy stood alone in the makeup area of the ladies room, trying to catch her breath. She put her hand over her heart, as if the gesture could calm the incessant pounding going on in there.

Her heart was palpitating, she was flushed and sweaty. If she didn't know better she would swear she was having a heart attack.

But it wasn't a heart attack. She was turned on.

Between Jake's kiss and the dance they'd just finished, she was a mix of pent-up emotion. He made her feel something. But what was it? Pure feminine ecstasy at having an attractive man showing interest in her, yes, but more than that. Plenty of good-looking men had pursued her, but they'd never captured her interest as much as Jake had.

Why him? They came from completely opposite ends of the social spectrum, and had nothing in common. And yet she felt a connection to him she'd never felt with another man.

Maybe it was physical. That short but oh-so-amazing kiss had sure made a physical impact on her. And dancing in his arms seemed a prelude to something more sensual, another type of dance, a different kind of rhythm. Visions she couldn't quite kick out of her head had haunted her during that dance. Every time he slid his hand over the bare skin of her back, or lightly flexed his fingers over hers, her mind flew to the various ways she'd want him to touch her.

None of this was good. They were playing a game, a charade. Their relationship was nothing more than a showcase to convince her father to back off. Guilt tugged at her middle, clenching like a fist. She was using Jake, and it wasn't fair.

But then again, this had been Jake's idea, and if she gained some freedom from her father's incessant pressure to marry, why not?

But what if she wanted more?

Did he want more?

As she stepped back into the ballroom, she scanned the bar for Jake. Her heart leaped to her throat when she found him surrounded by both her father and Alex. Lifting her skirts, she made quick work of catching up to them, hoping she could run interference before the two of them embarrassed Jake.

She arrived just in time to hear them arguing architecture. Obviously Jake knew building and construction, but she feared he was out of his league with an architectural discussion.

"You have to admit, the vertical concept and false fronts of the Italianates are truly a work of art," Alex said.

Raymond nodded smugly. "I agree. But the gingerbread carving strategy of the Eastlake style is really my favorite."

Jake hadn't uttered a word since she'd returned. He inclined his head in her direction, a hint of a smirk on his face, but other than that seemed content to let her father and Alex carry on.

Maybe he felt uncomfortable chiming in.

"Gentlemen," she said, hoping to steer the conversation away from grilling Jake, "I'm sure you'll all agree the fundraiser tonight has been wildly successful."

They all looked at her, nodded politely, then resumed their discussion as if she wasn't even there.

"The structure is astounding," Alex said. "Dalton, do you have any idea what type of wood was used to construct the early Victorians?"

Lucy rolled her eyes. What was this, a pop quiz?

"Some, I assume, were built with a prefabricated framework," Jake said. "However—"

"Really, gentlemen, I think what Jake's trying to say is—"

Her father waved his hand, silencing her interruption. "I believe you're mistaken, young man. Now, I understand someone like you could not possibly be aware of the history and architecture of our fine city."

Lucy was desperate to get Jake out of the line of fire. She stepped over to his side and tugged at his coat. "Would you like to dance?" she offered, giving him a visual signal that hopefully he'd see as rescue.

"Actually, what I was saying is entirely accurate." Jake stayed focused on her father, ignoring her completely.

"What do you mean?" Raymond asked.

Oh dear. Now he'd stepped in it. "I'm sure Jake was just making polite conversation. Really, Father, this inquisition is intolerable. Jake, let's go."

As if he hadn't heard her, Jake continued. "Some of these homes were built from prefabricated framework or plans that could be sent for in the mail, and others were planned and designed by architects. But most were made from redwood, which was available in abundance near the coast."

"True," Raymond stuttered. "But as far as the differing styles—"

Jake went on as if her father hadn't spoken. "While I can agree on you and Sheldon favoring the Italianate and Eastlake styles of Victorians, my favorite is the Queen Anne."

Lucy's jaw dropped.

"The Queen Anne's most distinguished feature is its steep gabled roof, a rounded turret corner tower, and a front porch usually inside the main structural frame. Some homes typically include a piece of each of the three mentioned styles, in which case they are referred to as San Francisco style. I tend to prefer the blended architecture because it showcases the finest aspects of all three."

Lucy was stunned. She'd finally stopped trying to figure out a way to extricate Jake, only to realize he was holding his own fabulously. The man knew architecture.

Her father and Alex tried a new tact. Politics. Followed by religion. And as they went on, attacking Jake's intelligence with difficult questions on global warfare, economics, finance, and the stock market, Jake answered every single one of them correctly.

They barraged him with questions, hoping to trip him up, to make him feel stupid. And he'd countered every single one of them with more knowledge about the subjects than she could ever hope to amass. In fact, he'd even put a few questions to them that neither her father nor Alex could answer.

With a sigh of relief, she relaxed. She'd underestimated Jake Dalton.

It didn't take long for Alex and her father to figure out they weren't going to be able to embarrass Jake, and they finally gave up in disgust, moving off to mingle with the politicians in attendance.

Lucy turned to Jake, about to tell him how impressed she was with his knowledge. But she was shocked at the fierce glare on his face. His jaw was clenched and his eyes narrowed. It didn't take a genius to figure out he was angry. Very angry.

At her. Without a word, he turned and headed to the door.

Lucy hurried after him, catching up to him near the front door of the hotel.

"Jake, wait!" She grasped his sleeve and fought to catch her breath.

He stopped, turned to her.

"Where are you going?"

"I'm going home, Lucy."

"Why?"

He didn't say anything for a minute. Then, "Why did you bother to bring me here tonight?"

"I don't understand."

"Did you think I was stupid?"

"No, no of course not." Frantically she tried to recall anything she'd said that he could have misinterpreted.

"If you thought I was so moronic that I couldn't enter into a simple discussion with your father and that idiot he parades around as your fiancé, then you shouldn't have asked me here."

Now she understood, guilt stabbing at her. "I didn't know how much you knew about the subject. Honestly, I was trying to spare you some embarrassment."

"I expected your father to treat me like I was stupid. I didn't expect you to feel the same way. I'm finished." He turned on his heel and walked through the doors.

Stunned, Lucy could only stare after Jake's retreating form, misery forming a knot in her stomach. What had she done?

He wasn't stupid. She was. She fled to the ladies room and flopped onto a chair, fighting back tears.

Jake had offered to help her out, and she had

insulted him. Underestimated his intelligence in a huge way. He was right. She *had* thought he wouldn't be able to hold his own in a conversation with Alex and her father, and he'd proved her, and them, wrong. He had a sharp wit and intelligence she hadn't expected.

And why hadn't she expected it? Because she had prejudged him based on his occupation. He was a construction worker, therefore he couldn't be as smart as lawyers, right? Blue jeans couldn't possibly hold their own against designer suits.

She bent over and laid her head in the palm of her hands.

For someone who'd always prided herself on not being one of the snooty upper class, she had sure shown her true colors tonight. She'd made judgments about Jake based on his social class, and not on him as a person. In doing so, she'd proved herself the biggest snob of all.

Jake threw the charcoal on the grill and ignited the flame, then picked up the slimy tennis ball his Golden Retriever, Rascal, had dumped on his foot.

"Don't you ever get tired?" he asked the dog, who sat at his feet, butt wiggling and tail flapping furiously back and forth. "Guess not."

He threw the ball across the yard as far as he could. Rascal took off in a determined gallop, growling and shaking his head when he pounced on his quarry.

Jake laughed at the dog's antics and headed inside for a beer. He walked past the pile of paperwork leering at him from the dining room table and chose to ignore it for the time being. It was Saturday, he was hungry, had been working on the house and yard all day, and he wanted a break. Paperwork could wait for later.

He'd thrown himself into home improvement projects since dawn, after spending a restless night tossing and turning. A vision of curly hair and eyes the color of pale jade haunted his dreams.

How could he have been so wrong about her? She'd seemed so unlike most of the upper class women he'd met before. Nonjudgmental based on what he did for a living. He thought she'd enjoyed his company on their date the other night. Then it turned out she was so deathly afraid he'd embarrass her in front of her father that she tried to steer him away from the conversation, certain he was too stupid to know the answers to the questions her father and Alex had asked him.

It was better to end things with her, anyway. Before he did something really moronic, like get involved. Like thinking she might care, that someone like her could actually fall for someone like him.

Lucy Fairchild was no better than his father. Passing judgment on him, condemning him as a failure for no good reason. He'd endured enough of that to last a lifetime.

Taking out his aggression by viciously tenderizing the steak with a wooden mallet, his annoyance ticked one notch higher at the sound of the doorbell.

Five o'clock on a Saturday. You'd think salespeople

would give a working guy a break and stay away on the weekends. He wiped his hands and stomped to the door, ready to skin alive the first person who tried to sell him something.

"What?" he said in a curt tone as he swung open the door.

Lucy blinked, taken aback by Jake's surly greeting. It was hard enough to be standing at his door, and with a welcome like that she felt like tucking her tail between her legs and running for her car.

"I'm...I'm sorry to bother you, Jake."

"How did you find my house?" he asked, frowning.

"You're listed in the telephone book." She'd been surprised to find how far outside the city he lived. Then again, considering the size of his house and yard, it didn't surprise her he had to travel half an hour east of San Francisco to afford this much land. Small houses with no yards went for over a quarter of a million in the city.

His brows knit together, but he didn't speak. Almost like he couldn't quite believe she was standing there.

"Jake?"

"Why are you here?"

This wasn't going to be easy. Did she really expect it to be? She'd just have to stand there and take it. Whatever he dished out, she deserved. "I'm here to apologize."

Somehow it didn't seem powerful enough. The words fell flat. He stared at her, his lips in a straight line, no emotion showing on his face.

"For what?"

"For last night. For what I did, for what I said. For assuming—"

"It's not necessary. You didn't need to come all the way out here."

"It is necessary," she said, taking a step toward him. He looked, as usual, amazing. Last night in a tux, today in shorts and a tank top, showing off tanned, broad shoulders. Her heart accelerated, whether from sheer nervousness or feminine delight she wasn't sure.

Taking a deep breath, she figured she'd better just spit it out. "Jake, I was wrong. I've always prided myself on not being a snob, not judging people based on their appearances or occupation. And I grossly underestimated you. I have no excuse other than complete stupidity. Please, I beg you to forgive me."

He stood silent for a moment, his head tilted at an angle as if digesting what she'd just said.

"Come in." He held the door open and motioned her inside.

With a silent sigh of relief, she stepped into the tiled entry, immediately struck by the simplistic beauty of his home. She'd thought the same thing when she pulled up into the double driveway. A one story beige frame with blue painted shutters and ornate double front doors, the house had beckoned her in welcome. The lawn was expertly manicured, evergreen bushes lined the picture window in the front, and three river birch trees provided a shady overhang.

Children played in the front yards of the surrounding homes, screaming and laughing, riding their bikes and playing ball.

It was a beautiful sight.

"You want a drink?"

She nodded and followed him, admiring the dark Berber carpet and pale gray walls. The furniture was modern, from the black leather sofa and matching chair in the family room off the entryway, to the glass and chrome table nestled in a nook in the kitchen.

"I've got beer, some white wine, or iced tea. Take your pick."

"A glass of wine would be great." She smoothed her hair off her face and tucked it into her ponytail before sitting down at the table.

He came back with a bottle of beer and a glass of wine. She took a sip, surprised at the smooth flavor.

"What is this?" she asked, twirling the liquid in the glass.

"Kendall Jackson Chardonnay, eighty-eight."

"I like it. Very easy and light."

He shrugged, but didn't respond.

"You have a lovely home," she said, cringing at the small talk.

"Thanks."

She turned at the sound of scratching, surprised to find a beautiful dog wagging its tail on the other side of the sliding glass door. “Oh! You have a dog!”

Without a look in Jake’s direction, she bounded from the chair and threw open the door, stepped out back and dropped to her knees to pet the dog.

He was very friendly, licking her face and wagging his tail furiously.

“Aren’t you just the sweetest thing?”

“His name’s Rascal.” Jake stepped out behind her.

She looked up at him. “He’s adorable.”

Jake rolled his eyes. “Wait ’til he drops his slimy tennis ball in your hand.”

Lucy laughed and ran her hands over Rascal’s thick coat. “I’ve always wanted a dog. I love animals.”

“Why don’t you have one?” He handed her glass of wine over and they sat at a white patio table with a blue flowered umbrella.

“Father would never allow it,” she said, petting Rascal on the head.

“So? Move out. You *are* kind of old to be living with Daddy, aren’t you?”

Not the first time she’d heard that. “I’ve thought about it, but Father and I spend so much time at night going over cases and paperwork related to the firm, I just felt it was easier to stay there. I have my own wing of the house, so I get plenty of privacy.”

“Uh huh.”

“Look, Jake. The house is huge. Father and I barely run into each other unless we’re having a meeting in the home office. We lead separate lives, and he stays out of my business."

At Jake's raised eyebrow, she added, "Mostly."

He leaned back in the chair and took a long swallow of beer. "And what if you want to bring a man home to spend the night? What then?"

Heat rose in her cheeks. "I don't."

"Ever?"

"No."

"So, you're a virgin."

"No!"

He laughed, and she felt her face flame even hotter.

"I meant I'd never bring someone to the house."

"What do you do when you want to sleep with someone?"

How had this conversation gotten so personal, so intimate? "I don't really think that's any of your business."

"Counselor, you're evading the issue."

"I'm not being evasive. I'm simply uncomfortable talking about something so personal."

"Your choice." He stood. "I'll be right back."

After he went into the house, Lucy took a couple quick drinks of wine and scrunched her shoulders, trying to ease the tension in her neck. She'd done what she came to do. They really had nothing left to say to each other.

Jake stepped back outside with a plate of steaks and layered them on the grill. Lucy giggled at Rascal's rapt attention to each slice of meat going from plate to grill.

"I really should go." She watched as he closed the lid on the grill and turned to her.

"You can't."

"Why not?"

"I just put a steak on for you."

"Oh." She supposed she'd been invited to dinner. "All right, then. Thank you."

"No big deal. We all have to eat."

Lucy hated this distance between them, and knowing she was the cause of it set the guilt demons plaguing her again. She wished she knew how to get things back the way they were before. Although they hadn't known each other long, she'd quickly grown accustomed to how comfortable she felt talking to Jake. There were no barriers, no games between them.

At least there hadn't been. Now there was a steel wall between them that she wasn't sure would ever come down. And she'd put it there.

"What can I do to help?" she asked.

After turning the steaks, he motioned her inside. "You can help me fix a salad if you want."

"I'd love to."

They stood side by side in the expansive kitchen. Lucy sliced vegetables at the counter while Jake prepared a potato dish on the stove. "You can cook, too?" she asked.

He smirked. "Yes, I can cook. I don't have servants to do it for me."

She bristled, feeling every sting of that insult. "Yes, we have servants. Should I apologize for that, too?"

"Not unless you feel it's necessary."

Instead of picking a fight, she held her tongue and took it out on the carrots and cucumbers, furiously slamming the knife into the poor, defenseless vegetables.

"Don't cut your finger off," Jake said over his shoulder. "I realize you probably don't have much experience with chopping vegetables."

That did it. She stormed over and grabbed his arm to turn him so he'd face her. "I screwed up last night. I realize that. I said I was sorry. If I have to go on apologizing for coming from a wealthy family, then I might as well leave now. Because I'll be damned if I'll allow you to make me feel guilty because of the circumstances of my birth. And you call me a snob? Well, you're a snob, too. You think just because I come from a rich family that I have no useful skills. Well, let me tell you, mister, I learned to cook a long time ago, I don't let the servants do everything for me. I can grocery shop, do the laundry, wield a dust rag and a broom as well as the latest in vacuum cleaners, and I mop a mean floor. So you can take your reverse snobbery and shove it."

She was so furious her entire body shook with the adrenaline rush it took to get that tirade out.

Jake's lips curled into a smile. He reached out a hand and gently extricated the knife from her fingers. She hadn't even realized she'd been pointing it at him the whole time.

"I'll take that." He seemed to be fighting a grin. "You sure get all fired up and passionate when you're pissed, don't you?"

"I'm sorry," she said, instantly mortified at her behavior. "I've never done anything like that before."

For the first time since she'd arrived, his eyes softened. "Hey. You're entitled to vent, too. And you're right. I guess I had a little leftover anger from last night."

"Truce?" she asked, holding out her hand.

He slipped his in hers and squeezed gently. "Truce."

Lucy sighed and went back to making the salad, feeling a considerable lightening in her heart.

Jake poured more wine and they worked together amicably, talking back and forth about her job and his. She set the table and put out the other food while Jake brought in the steaks. She smiled at the domestic scene. It was the first time she'd cooked with a man, and it felt good. Homey, comfortable—almost intimate.

Things between them felt right again. Which both thrilled her and scared the heck out of her at the same time.

What did *right* mean as it pertained to her and Jake? What was happening between them?

Something good? Or something that would end up hurting them both?

Chapter Five

Lucy pushed the plate away, completely satiated. After the huge dinner, coupled with two more glasses of wine, she couldn't move a muscle. A lethargic fog settled over her, and she figured she'd be stuck in the kitchen chair the rest of the night.

Jake held out his hand. "Come on, let's go out back and sit in the glider, watch the full moon."

Wrong. Not capable of movement. "I can't."

"Why not?"

"I'm stuffed and had too much wine. I'm immovable."

"You want me to sling you over my shoulder and carry you?"

"I'm up!" She stood, wobbled a bit, and followed Jake outside. When had the sun gone down? Dusky shadows fell over the moonlit backyard. They eased into the glider together, and Rascal settled at their feet.

Jake handed her yet another glass of wine.

"If I didn't know better, I'd swear you were trying to get me drunk so you could take advantage of me."

He slipped his arm over the chair, resting it lightly

against her back. His devilish smile held her. “Baby, if I wanted to take advantage of you, I’d make sure you were stone cold sober. I’d want you fully aware of everything that happened.”

“Oh.” She shivered with the promise of that statement, her mind conjuring up vivid images of naked limbs and fevered kisses.

She hoped she wasn’t drooling.

Time to change the subject to something neutral. “Tell me about your childhood.”

“Why do you want to know about that?”

“I’m interested.” She glanced at his profile silhouetted in the faint light from the kitchen window.

He gazed out into the darkness and took a sip of his beer.

“Not much to tell. I left home when I was sixteen, started working construction right after that.”

“You ran away?”

“Not really. My old man didn’t give a damn whether I stayed around or not. He was probably glad to see me go.”

She sensed the sadness wrapped around his carefully guarded words. “That must have been hard for you. What about your mother?”

“She died before I left.”

The bitterness in that statement brooked no further prodding. “I’m sorry.”

“It’s old history.”

“Still, it’s hard to lose a parent when you’re so young.

My mother died when I was six."

His hand slipped to her shoulder, and she felt the squeeze of his fingers against her bare flesh. "That's rough."

"I don't really remember much about her. I know she smiled a lot." Her memories were so distant. All she had were pictures of a laughing woman holding a young Lucy in her arms, looking for all the world like the happiest woman alive. She wished there were more.

"So, it was just you and your dad after she died?"

"Yes. He tried to be both parents, but Father isn't one for showing much affection. I know he loves me."

"Girls need a mom. Your dad never remarried?"

"No. He was too busy with work to even consider it. He never even dated after Mother died." Lucy wished he had. Maybe a woman's influence would have softened him. God knows she would have loved to have a mother figure around.

"Too bad. That's probably why you and your dad are so close."

Were they? Lucy wondered sometimes how her father really felt about her. He wasn't outwardly affectionate, and the only positive reinforcement she'd received when she was younger came upon making good grades in school. Even now, she'd get a pat on the back for winning a case at work. At times she felt more a valued employee than a beloved daughter.

"You and your dad? You didn't get along?" she asked.

Jake laughed. "That's an understatement."

"Why not?"

"He was a mean, vindictive, sorry SOB who never had a kind word to say to anyone in his entire life."

She turned to him and rested her hand on his. "That's a terrible way to raise a child. No wonder you left home."

"No big deal. I'm over it now," he said with a shrug and another pull of his beer.

Wanting to ask more questions, to delve deeper, she could tell by the distant look on his face that he didn't want to continue the discussion. "Did you finish high school?"

"Eventually. I hooked up with Bob and he kind of adopted me. Took me home with him. He and his wife, Shelly, gave me a place to stay. They never had kids, and I was trouble in the worst way, but still, they looked after me. Bob made me finish school before he'd let me work full time at the job sites."

Lucy warmed at the affection Jake showed for Bob. "Sounds like a very good man."

"He is. Pain in my butt sometimes, but he's been good to me."

"And now you have your own construction company. You've come a long way."

"I had to work damn hard to get here. Went to night school, again at Bob's not so subtle urging, while working full time in construction. Got my degree in business, continued to work like a madman, then had an opportunity to buy a company, so I took it."

"Do you have everything you wanted now?"

He stared straight ahead, his voice a near whisper. "Yeah. I have what I wanted."

"What about a wife and family? Is that on your list of things to do?"

He turned his head, his lips curving into a smile. "Haven't had time to even think about it."

She knew all about being driven and single minded. Working nonstop, constantly pushing. And what did she have to show for it? She was a partner in the family law firm. Big deal.

Her entire life had been spent fulfilling her father's dreams for her. Not once had she pursued her own. Now she stood at a crossroads, successful but not fulfilled. And she'd never taken the time to find someone she wanted to share her life with, to talk about having children with.

"What about you? Why aren't you married with a houseful of kids?" he asked.

She sighed. "Same reason, I guess. Wanting to prove myself, to be successful, and suddenly here I am, thirty years old. No husband, no children, not even any prospects. I hardly even date."

He laughed. "Aren't we a pair?"

"Yeah."

They grew silent and Lucy was glad. Their conversation reminded her of areas in her life that were lacking. Had a man ever told her he loved her? No. That would have been too momentous to forget. Not that she'd ever dated a man she wanted to hear those words from. The few relationships she'd had in the past were more to combat the occasional bouts of loneliness, to fulfill a social expectation, or to appease her father's constant need to find a suitable partner for her.

She'd never had that one, burning, passionate romance filled with love and promises of the future. And suddenly she ached for it, wanted it like she'd never wanted anything before.

Was it too late?

The night blessed them with a soft breeze, but she felt heated and restless. Maybe it was Jake's bare leg brushing against hers, the crisp hairs rubbing against her thigh. Maybe it was his hand lightly tugging at the loose curls at the back of her neck. She started to pull the mess back together in the ponytail.

"Quit doing that," he said.

"What?"

"Messing with your hair."

"I wasn't messing with it."

He laughed. "Yeah, you were. You do that a lot, you know."

"Really?" She resisted the urge to smooth her hair.

"Yeah. Your hair is gorgeous. Leave it alone. I like it a little messy." He pulled the pony tail holder off and slid his hands into the back of her hair, massaging her neck with his fingertips.

She shuddered at the sensual contact. His fingers worked magic, gently kneading the muscles.

“You’re tense. Turn around and I’ll rub your shoulders.”

She didn’t need to be told twice. She shifted sideways and presented him with her back.

The first touch of his strong hands was heaven. She hadn’t realized how much tension she’d been holding in.

He had such an expert touch. She felt like clay as he molded his thumbs to the knots, sliding along the tense spots until they melted away.

“You’re driving me crazy doing that,” he whispered in her ear.

“Huh?” She was so relaxed she was almost in a trance-like state, listening to the night sounds of crickets, Rascal’s light snore at her feet, and Jake’s breathing.

“You’re moaning.”

“I am?”

“Yeah.”

“Does it bother you?”

“Bothers the hell out of me.” His voice was low and husky and made her shiver.

She smiled into the darkness, feeling a tiny feminine thrill. She couldn’t recall ever driving a man crazy. It was an intriguing concept. “Your hands are magical.”

“You have no idea.” His hands traveled lower, gently pressing into the muscles of her back.

His touch weaved a tantalizing spell over her. Every nerve ending shot to life under his ministrations. She wanted his hands everywhere, wanted to feel his touch in other places besides her back.

Maybe it was the wine, or that she never relaxed, never let her guard down. Most men she knew were after one thing, and that was the Fairchild fortune. She was nothing more than a means to a merger. With Jake, it wasn't like that.

With him, she felt safe. Like he really wanted to be with *her*. Not because she was a Fairchild, but because she was Lucy.

How many times in her life had she taken a chance, taken the initiative? What would happen if she leaned back a little against Jake?

Feeling more than a little emboldened by the wine she'd consumed, she scooted toward him, her back half resting against his chest.

"What are you doing?" he asked, his voice suddenly tight.

"Getting more comfortable." What would she do if he pushed her away?

Shifting slightly, she half turned and placed her palm down on the glider on the other side of Jake. This put them nearly face to face. Her chest was inches from his chest. In fact, if she leaned in a little…

"Lucy."

"Yes?"

"You've got about five seconds to move away, or I'm going to hoist you on my lap and kiss you until your toes curl."

Fire burned from her already-curling toes to the top of her head. She struggled for her next breath, trying to find a way to bank the raging flames his hot words had sparked. Every second that passed, she knew she wanted that heat, that scorching flame.

"Okay."

In the light of the full moon his forehead wrinkled, his whiskey eyes darkened, and he swallowed. "Okay, what?"

Now was the moment. She could scoot away, maintain her distance, and keep things at the respectable level they'd been before. Or she could say the words and change their relationship. "Kiss me."

Without another word he pulled her roughly onto his lap, threaded both hands into her hair and pulled her face toward his. His mouth swooped down over hers, capturing it with the urgency of a starving man.

Her lips trembled at the first touch of his mouth on hers. Her breath caught on a sigh of exquisite pleasure as his tongue weaved its way inside, searching until it captured hers, tangling and twining in a heated frenzy.

This was no gentle kiss. This was hard, demanding passion, just as she expected. It was like the kiss he gave her in the bar that night, the kind of kiss she'd wanted ever since. Jake was not a tentative man in any way, and his kiss proved it. This was a man who knew what he wanted, and when he went after it, no holds barred.

Keeping one hand at the back of her neck, the other sloped down over her bare shoulder, sliding down her arm until he found her hip. He adjusted her closer, fitting her more intimately against him the same way his mouth held hers. Her hip brushed the hardened length of him, and heat pooled low and deep within her. She couldn't help pressing a little closer, rewarded by his guttural groan.

Breathing normally wasn't an option. She let loose a series of panting gasps as she caught her breath, desperate to touch him. She clenched at his shoulders, holding on to him as if she would fall.

Not a chance that would happen. Not the way he clutched her to him. She was practically on her side now, her legs drawn up against him, her breasts crushed against his heaving chest. She felt the mad thumping of his heart against her breasts, heard his groans of pleasure as he breathed against her mouth.

She uttered a protest when he tore his mouth away, but she was in ecstasy when he tilted her head back to rain kisses down her neck, licking the pulse point at her throat.

"Your heart's pounding," he said in a deep whisper.

"Yes," she rasped.

"I love your neck."

Goose bumps prickled on her skin at the feel of his tongue lathing the recesses of her throat. She slipped her hands into his hair, willing him closer, releasing a throaty laugh as his teeth nipped that spot between her neck and shoulder, lightly teasing the tender skin.

Jake turned the flame up a notch when he slipped his hand underneath her tank top, his palm grazing her ribs. Her stomach quivered at the glide of his fingers over her flesh. She'd never wanted a man's hands on her more than she did at that moment. He could have stripped her naked and had his way with her on the spot and she wouldn't make a single protest.

His hand snaked up the valley of naked skin from her belly to her ribs, resting on the spot just under her bra where her heart beat a frantic rhythm. Her nipples tingled and tightened under the flimsy silk, the only barrier to his questing fingers.

When his thumb swept over her breast she gasped and he once again captured her mouth in a long, drugging kiss. He lightly rubbed the palm of his hand over her aching nipple. It sprang to life, searching for the exquisite pleasure only Jake's touch could give. She arched her back, filling his hand with more of her.

Suddenly she was on her back across his lap, her neck resting in the crook of his arm. Their eyes met, his dark and smoldering like the incendiary feel of her body.

"Your skin is like butter," he said in a husky voice that pooled wetness between her thighs. He swept the tank top upward, baring her upper body to his greedy gaze. "I've wanted to look at you, to touch your skin and kiss you like this, since that first day you opened that sassy mouth of yours."

She should have been embarrassed lying in Jake's arms under a full moon, exposed like she was. But for some reason her sense of modesty had disappeared. Jake looked at her like she was the only thing in the world that mattered, a look she'd never seen on a man's face before. And whether it was reality or simply too much wine and stress, she didn't care.

All she knew was she didn't want the moment to end.

And then in an instant, she was sitting upright. Jake stood, combing his fingers through his hair.

What had just happened? Her body was awake and alive and dying for more, and he had suddenly stopped.

"What's wrong?" she asked, trying for some semblance of clarity. Her brain was fuddled and her body still lingered in a fog of sensual pleasure wrought from Jake's kisses and touch.

He blew out a breath, seemingly as shaken as she. The outline of his erection pressed rigidly against his shorts, telling her he was as affected as she was, and yet he had stopped from going further.

"I think we need a step back."

Maybe he wasn't as attracted to her as she'd thought. No—his body told her otherwise. "I'm confused. Did I do something wrong?"

"No. Hell, no. You didn't do anything wrong. I just fed you too much Chardonnay."

She tilted her head, trying to focus on his words. "Huh?"

He knelt in front of her, resting his hands on her knees. "You had a lot of wine tonight."

"Not that much."

"More than you think." He swept her hair away from her face. "We need to sober you up, clear your head. It's getting late. And if I'm going to make love to you, I don't want it to be because you're too fuzzy headed to know what you're doing."

The logical part of her heard what he said. The female part of her screamed in protest.

"Really, I'm fine." She stood, then wobbled a bit to the side. Okay, maybe she wasn't as fine as she thought.

"Yeah. You're fine all right. Let's get you up and moving around, breathing some fresh air."

How could she have had so much to drink? Lying in Jake's arms she'd felt fine. More than fine. Perfect, giddy, delirious with want and desire. That wasn't wine talking, then.

He slipped his arm around her waist and walked her around the stone patio, reminding her to breathe.

Ugh. Breathing was *not* making her feel better. In fact, she'd like nothing more than to curl up on the glider with Jake again. At least then her world hadn't been spinning out of control. Well, it had, but in a good way. She laughed at the thought.

"What's so funny?"

"Funny? I have no idea." What was she just laughing about? She couldn't remember.

"Breathe, Lucy. Take a deep breath. It'll help."

She did. It didn't. Now that she was actually up and

moving around, it hit her. Her legs wobbled.

“Oh. Oh, Jake, I don’t feel well at all.”

She tried to focus on Jake’s face, but suddenly there were two of him. He said something about green not really being her color, and then all hell broke loose.

Ten minutes later she was lying on the floor in his bathroom, praying for a quick death.

Chapter Six

Jake turned the door handle and pushed it open a crack to see if his overnight guest was still breathing.

He sucked in a breath at the scene before him. Lucy lay on her stomach with one arm flung over the side of the bed, her cute rear end stuck up in the air. Her hair was a mass of riotous curls, half swept over her face. She slept with her mouth open, too.

He swallowed, hard, thankful she at least had a cover on, considering she'd ripped her clothes off in his bathroom last night. That's how he'd tucked her in, trying not to look at her and muttering to himself about how much chivalry sucked.

After inching the door closed, he stepped into the kitchen and took a long drink of coffee, welcoming the jolting surge the caffeine provided.

Thank God he'd stopped last night. She wouldn't have, and if he hadn't had an inkling that she was tipping the scales on the drunk as a skunk side, he'd have had her right there and then. As it was, he'd entertained thoughts about pulling her astride him and letting her rock them both in the glider.

Instead, he'd had to stand by and watch her strip naked in his bathroom, then hold her hair while she'd emptied the contents of dinner and more than half a bottle of wine.

Not exactly a scene conducive to a passionate ending. After she'd given up everything she'd consumed, she curled up in a ball on the cold tile floor and promptly passed out. He'd cleaned her up, then carried her to his bed.

After he was certain she'd be all right, he'd flopped down in the spare bedroom, wide awake, achingly hard and unable to sleep. Remembering the feel of her in his arms. How perfect she felt there. Remembering her soft skin and pouty lips gliding over his, tearing him apart inside until he'd wanted to ravage her there in his backyard.

Probably a good thing he'd ended the kiss when he did. Otherwise he could have made a monumental mistake. Like making love to her. Him, the lowly toad, and her, practically a princess. Yeah, what a pair. A pair going nowhere.

Now he had a houseguest. A beautiful one. Sleeping naked in his bed. He'd give up a vital organ to join her there and feel the silk of her bare skin against his. He longed to touch his lips to hers again and slide his hands over her body until she moaned and begged for him to sink deep inside her. The thought of it brought on that familiar ache, the one he'd had nonstop since the first time he'd laid eyes on Lucy Fairchild.

"Mornin'."

Would it be inappropriate for a grown man to cry? Lucy stood at the doorway to the kitchen clad in one of his T-shirts. It skimmed her upper thighs and, though way too large for her, still made her look sexier than the night he'd seen her clad in black velvet.

"Good morning," he rasped, trying to find his voice. He took a swig of coffee and tried for a smile. "Feeling better?"

The pink tinge to her cheeks only added to her sexy look. She nodded and flipped her hair off her face. "Yeah. Much. I'm so sorry about last night."

He poured her a glass of ginger ale. "Sip this. Don't guzzle."

She took a couple sips and licked her lips, an action he watched with rapt fascination. "Thank you, I was thirsty."

"Dehydrated. Keep sipping."

She took a seat at the kitchen table, sliding her feet underneath her and pulling at the hem of his T-shirt. He bit back a smile and sat next to her.

"I take it I slept in your bed last night?"

"Yeah."

"And you slept..."

"In the guestroom."

"I'm so sorry." She dipped her head and fingered the hem of his t-shirt.

"Stop saying that. You think you're the first person to

drink too much and toss their cookies? Believe me, I'm the world's expert on overindulgence. I've just learned my limits."

She stared at the liquid swirling in her glass. "Obviously something I haven't done yet. I don't drink very often, and I guess I was so nervous last night I didn't realize how much wine I'd consumed until it was too late."

"Famous last words."

"Either way, I still feel I need to apologize. My behavior was appalling."

Jake leaned back in the chair and stretched his legs. "Maybe to those uppity people you associate with it would be. To someone like me, no big deal. Happens to a lot of people I know, myself included. Quit beating yourself up about it."

"So, did I do anything else, um, inappropriate last night?"

Her face held such a worried frown he didn't have the heart to laugh at her. "Inappropriate, how?"

Biting in her lower lip and then releasing it, she said, "I don't know, like streaking naked through your neighborhood or something equally horrendous?"

Jake crossed his arms and nodded, watching her eyes widen. "It was spectacular."

Her eyes widened. "I didn't."

"Truly, amazing feats of contortionism. I could go get the digital camera and show you the pictures I took, if you'd like." He made to stand.

She grasped his arm. “Jake, stop. I did no such thing. Did I?”

He laughed, and so did she.

“I should go,” she said.

“Let me fix you breakfast, first. You need something in your stomach.”

She wrinkled her nose. “I don’t think I ever want to eat again. I need a shower and a toothbrush.”

He inclined his head toward the hallway. “Go ahead. Extra toothbrush is in a package in the left hand drawer in the bathroom. By the time you get out I’ll have breakfast ready.”

She shook her head. “No, Jake. I appreciate it, but really, I think I’ve already overstayed my welcome.”

He stepped toward her and rested his hands on her shoulders. Knowing she was this close, knowing the only thing separating him from her naked body was a thin, gray T-shirt, had him hard in an instant.

“Go. Shower. No arguments.” And quickly. He had to get her out of there before she figured out he had ulterior motives. The physical evidence was becoming quite obvious.

“Fine,” she said with a curving smile and turned quickly, padding down the hall. He watched her progress, bare feet shuffling along the carpet and backside swinging in a naturally provocative way.

With a groan, he plopped down in the kitchen chair and laid his head in his hands. Chivalry. What idiot thought that one up?

Lucy stood under the pulsating heat of the glass-blocked shower, luxuriating in the cleansing sensation of rinsing away the horror from last night. She felt one hundred percent better. Almost human, in fact.

Her mind was still a little unclear. Fortunately, the things she'd forgotten were the unpleasant moments, after she had gotten sick. She remembered quite clearly being cradled in Jake's arms and sharing some intensely hot kisses.

He'd touched her, caressed her skin with his bare hands. She'd wanted more. A lot more. But then he'd stopped.

At least one of them had some common sense, and it hadn't been her. She'd gone into this so-called relationship with Jake intending to do nothing more than parade him around as her boyfriend of the moment so that she could get her father to mind his own business and maybe let her make her own choices for once.

Instead, she'd been taking this whole thing way too seriously. Like she really was having a romance with Jake. Which was ludicrous.

Wasn't it?

Reluctantly she turned off the shower and stepped out, grabbing an oversized bath towel and tucking it around her. Her nipples tightened at the thought of Jake's body wrapped in this very towel. Apparently she was feeling better since her thoughts ran rampant with visions of a naked Jake in the bathroom.

Now what? First things first. She needed to find her things. A vague recollection of flinging her clothes while ill last night came back to her. She glanced at her mortified face in the mirror.

She'd stripped in front of Jake.

Dear God, why couldn't episodes of idiocy be wiped from one's memory forever? Instead, the bits and pieces were coming back to her in all their horridly vivid glory.

He'd held back her hair while she'd thrown up. No one had ever done that for her, not even her father when she was a child. When she'd been sick, he'd sent servants to deal with her illnesses.

The sudden welling of tears caught her off guard, and she leaned against the counter, feeling for all the world like Jake was the first person to ever care for her.

Except he didn't care for her. Yes, he had proved himself to be a gentleman, much more than she could have expected considering her behavior last night. But his actions belied the impression she'd had of a rough, didn't give a fig about anybody, type of man.

Preconceived notions again. Just because he wasn't from her social world didn't mean he couldn't care. He had shown her more heart in the week she'd known him than most people she'd known her entire life.

In less than a half hour she had found her clothes, combed through her wild nest of hair, and at least felt presentable enough to exit the bathroom. Jake was in the kitchen. The smell of coffee and bacon got the hunger juices flowing in her stomach.

Jake was right. She did need to eat.

"Smells wonderful."

"Sit down, it's ready." He carried two plates filled with eggs, bacon and toast to the table, where coffee and juice had already been poured.

"You didn't have to go to all this trouble." She felt guilty that she hadn't even helped.

"It's no trouble. I have to eat, too."

She dove into the food, her appetite returning with a vengeance. After they finished, she jumped up and cleared the table, ran some water and washed the dishes. At least that made her feel somewhat useful.

"Wow. You know how to clean up," he said behind her.

She turned, ready to throw the dishrag in his face when she caught his lifted brow and casual smile. "Funny. Yes, I've watched the servants do it a hundred times. Seemed like a piece of cake so I thought I'd try it for fun."

He laughed, and then his smile died. "Lucy, I need to talk to you about something."

Oh no. Not right now. Not when she felt comfortable, relaxed, even happy. She didn't want to hear his regrets about last night. She didn't need to hear him say it was a mistake—she already knew it.

"Wow. Look at the time. I really have to go." She pushed past him without another word and grabbed her purse.

"But, I—"

"Thanks for last night, Jake. And for breakfast. We'll talk again soon," she said, effectively cutting off his next sentence. She almost ran, in her haste to get out the front door.

Once in the safety of her car, she exhaled, gripping the steering wheel with both hands. Stupid, stupid, stupid. What kind of a coward was she, anyway? They could have talked about last night like adults, admitted it was an error in judgment, and laughed it off. Instead, she had run.

Fearless Fairchild never ran away. What was wrong with her?

Something was seriously wrong. Lucy tapped her pen against the blotter on her desk and stared at the deposition, not really reading the words on the page. She crossed her legs and swung her foot back and forth, trying to calm the unexplained nervous jitters plaguing her.

She swiveled in the chair and focused on the cherry bookshelves to the side of her desk, lined with books on case law. No, nothing there to spark her interest.

Turning halfway, she looked out the window at the fog-enshrouded Golden Gate Bridge. The afternoon sun was nearly obliterated by the rolling cloud of white sweeping in from the Pacific.

A cloud. That's where she'd been for the past three

days. She hadn't heard from Jake since the day she ran out of his house. Of course, she hadn't bothered to pick up the phone and call him, either. When she made her daily trek down the street for coffee, she could have stopped in at the trailer. But she hadn't.

He was probably grateful she'd left him alone. She could imagine what he must think of her—a spoiled socialite who over-imbibed and threw herself at a man who wasn't remotely interested.

No, that wasn't quite right. He *had* been interested, at least physically. She'd felt the hard evidence of his interest pressing against her hip. But somehow she got the impression he thought she was way more trouble than she was worth.

He was probably right.

This whole charade had been a mistake from the very beginning, anyway. Best that it didn't go any further.

So why did she miss him? Why hadn't she been able to concentrate on work for the past three days? Why did every thought upon waking and retiring center around a tall, gorgeous man with whiskey eyes and a smile that could thaw a polar bear's heart?

"Lucille, we need to talk."

She jumped at the sound of her father's voice. Damn. He'd been out of town the past couple days, and she'd avoided his calls, knowing the inquisition that would inevitably follow.

Her father shut the door to her office and slipped into one of the dark leather chairs in front of her desk. "You've been unavailable."

"Yes, I have. Sorry. Working on a case."

He frowned. "The Marshall case isn't due for trial for six weeks."

"I'm preparing in advance."

"Bah," he said with a dismissive wave of his hand. "You don't need to prepare. You're avoiding me."

"I am not. I told you, I've been busy."

"Where were you Saturday night?"

Here it comes. "Out."

"With whom?"

"With none of your business."

"Why didn't you come home?"

"It was late and I didn't want to make the drive."

"Where were you?"

"Out of town."

"Again, with whom?"

Why did it always seem like she needed her own lawyer present whenever her father badgered her with questions? She felt like she was giving a deposition.

She leaned forward on her desk and looked her father in the eye. "For the record. On the night of Saturday, June twenty-fifth, I, Lucille Fairchild, was out doing whatever I wanted with whomever I wanted to do it with. The details of said evening are private, personal, and once again, none of your business."

"I'm worried about you, Lucy."

She pursed her lips and inhaled, so familiar with this routine it was laughable. When he didn't get his way playing stern father, he resorted to endearments and soft words. It used to work. Not anymore. "Don't worry about me. I'm fine."

"You're still seeing that construction worker, aren't you?"

"Father, this may come as a shock to you, but I'm thirty years old and no longer required to report to you about my private life."

"You've changed." He stood and walked to her window, his hands clasped behind his back.

Ah, yes. First stern boss, then concerned father, followed by disappointed parent. So predictable.

"No, I haven't." If he'd ever bother to notice her he'd see that. She was the same person she'd always been. Deep inside, there still lurked a lonely little girl desperate for affection from her father.

He turned his head toward her. "Why are you wasting your time on someone with whom you have nothing in common?"

"Father, I'm not going to discuss my boyfriends with you."

He raised a brow. "Boyfriend, is it? Then I take it things have escalated between you two?"

There was a reason Raymond Fairchild was a master litigator. She'd always had to be careful what she said in front of him. He had a unique way of twisting her words around until she had to defend herself. Well, she was her father's daughter, and just as good as he at manipulating words and evasion.

"Not your business."

Silence. That meant he was thinking. Plotting. Devising new ways to attack. She mentally prepared herself for what would come next.

The door to her office flew open and her secretary, Maggie, rushed to her desk.

"Stud alert," Maggie said in a breathless whisper, her cheeks flushed almost as red as her hair.

"Excuse me?"

"Oh, my God, Lucy. There's this incredible-looking guy in the reception area and he just asked for you. What a hunk of man!"

A cough sounded behind Maggie, and she whirled, her face reddening instantly. "Oh! Mr. Fairchild, I am *so* sorry. I didn't know you were in here."

"It's quite all right, Miss Sims," her father said with a straight face. "And who is this gentleman to see Lucille?"

"Uh, a Mr. Jake Dalton, I believe he said his name was," Maggie stammered, then threw Lucy a panic-stricken look.

Lucy hid a smile behind her hand. "Thank you, Maggie. Would you show him in?"

Maggie made a quick exit and Lucy stood, her hand on the door. "If you'll excuse me, Father." She hoped he'd take the hint and leave before Maggie brought in Jake.

"I'm not leaving."

"Yes, you are."

Too late. Maggie arrived at the door, Jake behind her. One look at him and Lucy's heart pounded and her palms began to sweat. He must have come right off the job site. Construction dust clung to his jeans, and his work shirt bore dark stains. Wow. Did he look hot.

Maggie stepped aside to let Jake in the office. Spying her father, Jake leaned over and pressed a light kiss to Lucy's lips. Her feet melted to the floor.

"Hey, babe," he said with a wink before turning to her father and raising his hand. "Mr. Fairchild."

Lucy looked to her father, who ignored Jake's outstretched hand, shook his head and stormed from the office.

Jake shrugged and stepped in.

Maggie lingered at the doorway, her mouth hanging open. Lucy told Jake to have a seat and then looked toward Maggie. "That'll be all, Maggie. And close your mouth."

"Oh. Sorry. But, wow, Lucy, he's fine."

Lucy couldn't help but beam, knowing exactly how Maggie felt. "Yes, he certainly is. Hold my calls, please."

With a vacant nod, and a dreamy smile on her face, Maggie walked away and Lucy closed the door.

"Hi," she said as she sat in the chair across from Jake, her mind stuttering for something to say. Just looking at him occupied every brain cell.

"Hi, yourself. Nice office."

"Thanks."

His gaze traveled the length of her. "Sexy as hell little suit, too."

She looked down at the navy blue pinstripe, wondering what he found sexy about a basic two-piece suit. Though she warmed considerably at his compliment.

"Thanks. Sexy as hell jeans and T-shirt, by the way."

He laughed. "Thanks."

Why was he here? And why couldn't she manage to open her mouth and ask? She was way too old to be rendered tongue tied by a guy, wasn't she?

"What brings you here today?"

He shifted a bit in the chair and stretched his legs, then glanced at the door. Was Jake Dalton nervous? That had to be a first.

"You ran out the other day before we could talk."

"Yes, I know. Sorry." What was she supposed to say? That she'd been too scared he'd tell her he didn't want to see her again? Sheesh. It really was time to grow up.

"I wanted to ask you a question."

Gulp. "Okay."

"There's a thing coming up next weekend."

"A thing?"

"Yeah. Kind of an event."

A thing which was an event. Now that was vague. "Could you be more specific?"

He *was* nervous. He lifted and lowered his shoulders

and sighed. “Uh, every year the contractors host a barbecue, picnic kind of thing. All the company owners attend.”

“Okay.” She was an expert at pulling information out of witnesses, surely she could do the same with Jake. “And?”

“This year it’s at my house.”

She crossed her arms and tried to hold back a smile. “Which means?”

“I’ve never hosted it before, since I was never a company owner.”

“You must be very excited.”

He rolled his eyes. “Hardly.”

She wasn’t a rocket scientist but she was getting the gist of where the conversation was going. “Would you like me to help you?”

With a dramatic sigh, he nodded. “Would you? God, I hate to ask, and if there were anyone else I wouldn’t.”

“Oh, gee, thanks a lot.”

“Ah, hell. That’s not what I meant at all.” He jammed his hand through his hair. “I’m not handling this well, am I?”

“You’re doing fine, Jake.” She found the entire conversation endearing, and more than a little eye opening. He needed her help.

“Okay, anyway. I have no idea what to do. I mean, I can barbecue, but the whole entertaining thing is way out of my league. There’s going to be husbands and wives and kids and we can't stand around staring at each other all day. I'm not good at planning entertainment. I don't want it to be fussy, but I don't want everyone to be bored, either."

"Relax." She leaned over and laid her hand on top of his, feeling the sun-warmed heat of his body. "I've been handling social affairs for my father for years now. I'll be happy to help you."

"Thanks. I really appreciate it."

She stood and grabbed her pad and pen from the desk. "Okay, first things first—the menu."

Chapter Seven

The party turned out perfectly, even if she said so herself. Lucy stood outside under the tent they'd erected this morning, watching the crowds mingle at the food table. She mentally checked off her list, trying to figure out if she'd missed anything.

Not a thing. There were ribs, burgers, and hot dogs for the main food choices. Then they had potato salad, fruit salad, corn on the cob, jello salad and coleslaw. Buns, slices of bread, and all the condiments. And drinks, from soft drinks to beer and wine.

She'd passed on the wine. Iced tea for her today. This wasn't a day for a repeat of her previous performance.

Jake had told her to keep it simple. He'd warned her this group of people wouldn't find caviar and pate to their liking. She'd sneered at his laughing face, telling him she knew how to plan a party to fit the guests.

Although she had to admit to having experienced a bout of nervousness before everyone arrived this afternoon. Worried about every little detail, wanting this party to be successful for Jake, had her pacing the yard like a caged tiger.

Jake finally had to tell her to stop obsessing, that everything looked perfect, she'd done a wonderful job, and she could relax and enjoy the party.

Little did he know. The hostess never really enjoyed the party, they were too busy making sure everyone else had a good time.

They'd gone with picnic tables and benches so they could seat more people. Thankfully, Jake had a huge backyard, easily accommodating the thirty or so guests along with their children, with plenty of room to set up a game area for the kids. She had an inflatable bouncy house brought in for the little kids to romp around in, and a trampoline for the older kids, which they loved. Even a few of the more daring adults had ventured onto it once or twice today.

The best part of the day had to be the children. They were all adorable. They ranged in age from six months old to twelve. She'd told Jake there was nothing more boring than to drag a child to a stuffy party where nothing was set up for them to enjoy. So she'd made sure there were plenty of activities for them, no matter their age.

The last thing she wanted was to have the children endure what she'd had to. Endless social engagements more fitting for adults than children. No other kids to play with. Her father hadn't had the first clue what to do with a child. She'd been his companion and hostess at parties from the time she was old enough to talk.

He told her the best way to teach her about the family business was to expose her to it. So while other girls her age were playing with Barbies, she'd been taught to play the "who's sitting on the Supreme Court" game.

Not today, though. Today was a day for fun and games, both for the adults and the children.

So far, so good. The kids were having fun, the adults were milling and enjoying, and she hadn't had a moment to even speak to Jake in about two hours. Which pretty much left her surrounded by a bunch of strangers.

Not that it mattered. This was the friendliest group of people she'd ever had the pleasure to meet. The women didn't raise their eyebrows at her presence there with Jake, instead welcomed her as if they'd known her for years. She just hoped she didn't get anyone's name wrong.

"You've done a wonderful job today, Lucy."

She turned and smiled at Bob's wife, Shelly. "Thank you, Shelly. I hope everyone's having a good time."

Shelly beamed, her rosy cheeks plumping up with her grin. "You can bet on it. The rest of us will have a hard time making our turns as spectacular as this one."

Lucy frowned. "Too much, you think?"

"No, not at all." Shelly laid a hand on her arm. "It's perfect. Just what this stodgy old group needed. And we're thrilled there's something for the kids to do."

"Speaking of kids, I need to go make a call. Can someone hold Bayley?"

One of the contractors' wives, Lucy thought her name was Maria, handed off the infant into Lucy's arms.

She couldn't recall ever holding a baby before. Not having any brothers or sisters or relatives with children meant her exposure to babies and small children was, well, nil.

But she cradled Bayley in her arms. The infant looked up at her, smiled a toothless grin, and promptly drooled all over Lucy's chest.

"She likes you," Shelly said.

"She's adorable," Lucy countered, feeling a maternal urge to protect this child unlike anything she'd ever experienced. Was that a natural feeling? Did all women feel this way?

"You look good with a baby. Thinking of having your own any time soon?"

Jake had warned her Shelly would be the worst at matchmaking. He'd told her that as soon as Shelly and the rest of the women found out they were dating, they'd have a wedding date set before Lucy could utter a word.

He was nearly right.

"Um, yes, I've thought about having children, of course." Lucy kept her eye on Bayley, who found her silver necklace fascinating, flicking the dangling beads on the chain with her chubby, wet finger. "I'll need to focus on finding a husband first."

Shelly laughed. "Honey, with your looks and that body, I can't imagine you'd have much trouble."

Lucy felt her cheeks warming. "Thank you. You'd be surprised how difficult it is to find a good man."

"You might have already found one. Jake is a prize that many women have tried to claim for themselves."

"Really?" Lucy looked around, trying to find Jake. She didn't see him.

"Really."

Shifting Bayley in her arms, she and Shelly took a seat on the glider. The baby sat forward in her lap, and found Rascal to be quite entertaining. Every time he licked her hand she'd pull it back and giggle.

Trying not to think too hard about what happened the last time she'd been in the glider, she turned to Shelly. "Does Jake date a lot of women?"

She immediately felt guilty for asking the question, knowing she was prying into Jake's personal life, but curiosity got the better of her.

"Not really. Like I said, he's had plenty of offers, and he goes out now and then. But he spends way too much time on business if you ask me. Not like he's getting any younger, and I need grandchildren."

Lucy laughed at Shelly's comment. "Kind of see yourself as his pseudo-mother, do you?"

She nodded. "Poor boy had it rough the first part of his life. I'm just glad he ended up with Bob and me. We'd always wanted children, but it never happened for us."

"I'm sorry." Lucy looked at Shelly now, still a beautiful woman though she had to be well past sixty. She wore her hair in a stylish chin-length cut, and it was a thick, gorgeous silver. Lucy'd give her right arm for straight, sleek hair like that.

"It's okay. We long ago accepted it. And I think God had a plan for us. We were needed to take care of Jake. He's more my son than any other child I could have ever given birth to."

The woman's obvious love for Jake warmed Lucy. "Jake's a very lucky man."

Shelly's brown eyes glittered with happiness. "Thank you. But now, like a concerned mother, I want to see him as happy as Bob and I have been all these years."

"I'm sure it's just a matter of time before the right girl comes along." Why, as soon as she uttered the words, did she feel a stab of jealousy? It wasn't like she was going to be the girl of Jake's dreams. And yet, the thought of him sitting on this glider with another woman brought about a fierce emotion. Anger? As if he were cheating on *her.* As if he were *hers* and no way was she going to let another woman get her claws in him.

"Maybe he's already found the right girl."

Lucy stared at Shelly's knowing smile, and shook her head. "I don't think so."

"Maybe you're not as smart as I thought you were, then," Shelly said with a pat on Lucy's shoulder.

A couple of the other kids stopped at the glider to talk to Lucy and play with Bayley, effectively cutting off further conversation with Shelly. Good thing, too, since she didn't have an appropriate comeback for Shelly's last statement.

Jake found Lucy sitting on the glider with Shelly, holding Maria's baby in her lap and surrounded by kids like a shepherd with her flock. Seeing her like that struck him immobile, his heart skipping a beat.

Her face was flushed, her head thrown back, exposing that neck that begged for his teeth, and she was laughing at something one of the children said to her.

One thing he'd discovered over the years was that kids could spot a phony or someone who didn't naturally love children. Kids avoided adults who didn't like them. They'd been hanging on Lucy all day long, and not once had she frowned at them, told them she was too busy, or otherwise given them the brush off. Each time one of the kids pulled the hem of her shorts she'd stopped whatever she was doing, bent down to their eye level, and gave them her full attention.

His heart felt mushy, and that had never happened to him before.

He never got mushy. That was for women, or men who were too weak to hide their emotions. What the hell was happening here?

All he knew was that he hadn't had a moment alone with Lucy all afternoon, and he didn't like it one bit. Granted, he was the host and besides handling the barbecue, he also had to play bartender and handle some PR with his peers. But dammit, the one thing he wanted was in his line of sight but out of his reach.

And the way things were going, it didn't look like he'd be able to grab a minute alone with her for some time to come.

Not that he was sure what he wanted to do if he had that minute with her, but he'd damn sure think of something.

"Your girl is spectacular."

Jake turned and smiled at Maria Sampson. He'd known her husband, Steve, since they'd apprenticed together on his first job site. Steve had been four years older but as green as Jake.

"Thanks."

"She's great with Bayley."

He followed Maria's gaze to see Bayley pulling herself to a standing position by grabbing on to Lucy's blue top, which appeared to be sliding further down her chest, nearly revealing her perfect breasts. Lucy just laughed, gently extricated Bayley's hand from inside the top, and held on to the baby's little fingers so she could stand.

"Yeah. She's great."

"Good choice, Jake," Maria said. He watched as she went over and rescued Lucy from Bayley's chubby clutches. Lucy looked as if she was reluctant to let the baby go.

There it was again, that tugging on his heart. Oh, man, he needed a drink. And maybe a stiff dose of some angry testosterone before he ended up dropping to his knees in front of Lucy and begging her to marry him and bear his children.

Wouldn't she get a laugh out of that one?

Thankfully, he spent the next hour busily feeding everyone and cleaning up the mess. By the time dusk rolled around, most of the group was ready to head home.

Jake was more than ready for them to be gone.

Thank God Lucy had planned this party. One by one everyone had congratulated him and told him it had been the best contractors' barbecue yet. But he wasn't about to take the credit. Left up to him, they'd have had hot dogs, beans and beer, and would have spent the entire day sitting around and staring at each other.

Lucy had saved his butt.

"She sure saved your behind today," Bob said, coming up to stand next to him. They both watched Lucy play a round of some kind of Nerf ball game with the kids. She looked to be having as much fun as the children. Her eyes would go wide over some antic, then she'd giggle uncontrollably, finally ending up with two or three little ones tumbling on top of her.

Jake bit back a groan at watching her writhe all over the ground, her slender legs exposed in her little shorts. What he wouldn't give to join her and really give her a reason to roll around.

He popped open the can of beer and took a couple quick gulps, thankful for the cooling liquid on his parched throat. Figured today would be the hottest day of the summer so far. Fortunately, Lucy had anticipated it and suggested the tents to keep the sun away.

Face it. She'd thought of everything.

"Shelly really likes her. Hell, all the women like her. Nobody had an unkind word to say about her." Bob looked at Jake and shrugged, almost as if he was sorry to be the bearer of that news.

Didn't surprise Jake in the least. He'd been busy today, but not too busy that he didn't notice the way she fit in with his crowd. Not that he'd worried she wouldn't. Well, maybe a little. Funny how she could be so at ease with his kind of people, when he expected her to be bored or appalled at the behavior of the kids.

"I'm glad Shelly liked her." Her opinion meant a lot to Jake. Shelly had called him on some of the women he'd brought around over the years, and damn if she hadn't been right about every one of the women she'd told him were a complete waste of his time.

"I gotta warn you," Bob said, "she's already thinking of you two as a permanent couple."

Jake rolled his eyes. "Not gonna happen."

"You sure?"

"Yeah, I'm sure."

Bob's snicker didn't go unnoticed. Nor did his mumbled "famous last words" as he walked away.

No. It wasn't gonna happen. Not now, not ever. So he might as well get any heart tugging, thinking of Lucy as goddess of creation, out of his head, because their worlds were not going to collide.

Trouble was, they already had. Every day he spent with her she wriggled more and more into his head, his mind and his heart. He had to get her out of there, and fast. To her, this was just a charade. If he got attached to her he was going to lose.

Hell, he'd already lost. Everyone had left, finally, and he stood at the back door, mesmerized while watching that perfect backside of hers as she bent over to pick up trash. Little blue shorts stretched tight, along with that clingy top that showed just a hint of cleavage along with some blue, lacy-looking bra.

He adjusted his shorts, feeling the almost instantaneous twitching which always occurred whenever she was around.

Thankfully he had been too busy today. Wouldn't have looked too good to have his peers see him follow Lucy around the yard, drooling like a dog on a too hot summer day.

She finally turned and spotted him, then straightened and graced him with a brilliant smile that he could see despite the gathering darkness. He walked toward her.

"You don't have to clean up," he said, taking the trash bag from her hands.

She frowned. "I don't mind. Besides, there's not much left to do. Most everyone put all their trash in the bags."

They patrolled the yard together, Lucy clearing off the last of the cans and paper plates that had been left, while Jake held open the trash bag. He kind of liked this domestic stuff. Surprisingly, she hadn't complained once about doing any of the prep work or the clean up.

For a stuck-up socialite, she sure seemed to enjoy the down home simplicity of his life.

Or maybe he was reading into this what he wanted to

see, not the way things really were. She was simply being polite because he'd asked for her help. Nothing more than that.

"I think we got it all picked up," she said, sweeping her hair away from her face. She stood in the middle of the yard, hands on hips, and nodded.

They headed into the house and Jake fixed them both a drink, then motioned for Lucy to join him in the living room. They sat on the leather sofa, which felt cool to his legs after the itching heat from outside.

"Thank you for helping. Thanks for everything today. I couldn't have done this without you."

A blush stained her cheeks. "It was fun. I didn't mind at all. Do you think it turned out okay?"

"Hell yeah. From what I heard it was the hit of all the barbecues so far." He stretched his legs on the coffee table in front of him. "Everyone said they'd have a hard time competing with this one."

"Oh, it wasn't that big a deal. Just a few bites of food and some games for the kids."

She looked beautiful sitting there, her expression tentative, yet hopeful. For someone with so much going for her, she sure seemed a mass of insecurities. Didn't she realize how great she was?

Reaching out, he grabbed a loose curl and threaded it through his fingers.

"You did more than just a little. Take a bow, you deserve it. And I really appreciate your help."

"You're welcome. I actually had a great time today."

"I could tell. You seemed to really enjoy the kids," he said, trying to find some way to break the spell she wove over him.

She grinned. "I love being around kids. I wish I had more exposure to them, but unfortunately, not many of the people I know have children. The social events I attend don't allow kids."

"You know, you looked completely different out there today. Nothing like a lawyer at all."

One corner of her mouth lifted in that saucy grin he liked so much. "Really? And what did I look like?"

He thought a moment, and then it struck him. The way the children gravitated to her, her natural ability to make them feel comfortable. "You looked more like a kindergarten teacher."

Her face paled and the smile died on her face. Tears pooled in her eyes, threatening to spill over.

"Hey. What's wrong?"

She shook her head. "Nothing. I'm sorry, it's just that I, what I mean is, what you said, oh, never mind. I'm sorry, please excuse me."

Her last words were said on a quivering gasp. She set her glass on the table and literally ran into his bathroom, slamming the door shut behind her.

Jake sat there, stunned and confused.

What the hell had he said to set her off like that?

Chapter Eight

Lucy sniffled and blew her nose, dreading the moment she'd have to leave Jake's bathroom.

What an idiot she was, falling apart like that in front of him. Poor guy probably had no idea what had caused her flood of tears. He was most likely blaming himself right now for some imagined transgression. She really should get out there and let him know her meltdown had nothing to do with him.

As soon as her face looked less blotchy and her nose didn't light up as red as a certain Christmas reindeer's. Lord, she looked dreadful.

"Lucy?"

She whirled around at the knock at the door and the sound of Jake's voice. "Yes?"

"Are you okay?"

"I'm fine." She sniffed.

He was quiet for a moment and she thought he'd left, until he said, "Uh, are you gonna come out any time soon?"

Not if she could help it. How was she going to explain

what just happened? Chalk it up to PMS? Discussion of anything female usually resulted in the man wanting to end the topic of conversation immediately. That could work.

She turned to the mirror, scrunched her face at her reflection, and proceeded to the door, opening it with a smile.

The look of genuine concern on Jake's face was enough to make the tears well all over again.

"Are you sure you're all right?"

"I'm great." She opened the door and stepped out into the hall. "Just a bout with PMS, I think."

Yes, that definitely worked. The look of horror on his face was almost laughable. She bit her lip to suppress a threatening giggle. "Shall we go back to the living room?" she suggested.

"Nah, I've got a better idea. Come with me."

Jake grabbed her hand and led her through the kitchen to the backyard. Lucy gasped when she saw what he'd done.

Lit candles sat on the ground near the oversized trampoline, where Jake had thrown a pile of blankets. When she turned to him, he smiled.

"Might be some shooting stars tonight, according to the forecast. Thought we might relax out here and stare at the sky for awhile."

When she didn't say anything, he added, "You know, relax and unwind a bit? It was a pretty hectic day."

Just like that, with no mention of her tearful exit earlier. "It sounds great. I'd love to."

They headed over to the trampoline. Before she could climb on, Jake scooped her up in his arms and easily lifted her onto the wiggly apparatus. After a few seconds she managed to balance enough to make it to the center of the trampoline. He jumped on and joined her.

He'd spread out a couple sleeping bags on the bottom and added a few folded blankets for them to cover up with. She shivered, and he reached under the blanket for a sweatshirt.

"Here, put this on. It's kind of cool now that the sun's gone down."

She took the offered sweatshirt and balanced on her knees in order to put it on. It hung way below her shorts and smelled spicy clean, just like Jake. She couldn't resist the urge to hug his garment next to her before settling in on the blankets.

"You'll have to lay down to see, otherwise you'll get an ache in your neck."

Following his lead she lay on her back. He pulled the blankets over them both and settled in next to her.

Try as she might to focus on the stars, the man next to her grabbed all her attention. She listened to the sound of his even breathing, intensely aware of his warm body fitted so closely against hers. How would they feel nestled up against each other, her leg wrapped over his, her head resting on his chest?

And how would he react if she threw herself on him

like that? Would he bolt, or would he welcome her in his embrace?

How many times over the past couple weeks had she thought about what it would be like to lie naked next to him? She'd caught glimpses of his strong, muscled body, and many times thought about that body covering hers in passion.

Why was she even thinking these thoughts? They weren't even really dating. Sure, she'd come to think of Jake as a friend, someone she felt comfortable around. But as a lover, a potential partner? No. He wouldn't be happy in her world, and her family and peers would never welcome him. And that she'd never put him through.

Not that he'd be interested, anyway.

She laughed at the way her mind wandered.

"What are you laughing about?"

"Oh. Um, nothing. My mind was wandering."

"About?"

How would he react if she told him what she'd really been thinking? "I was thinking about a case I'm taking to court next week."

"Oh."

Idiot. She had to blast these thoughts of her and Jake into orbit, shoot them across the sky like the stars they were watching, until the thoughts disappeared out of sight.

And out of her mind.

"Can I ask you a question?" he asked.

"Sure."

"What happened in there? What did I say that upset you?"

She knew it had been too good to be true. Hoping that he'd forget about the incident didn't mean it was going to happen. Now she'd have to face it.

"You said I reminded you of a kindergarten teacher."

"Yeah, and?"

"It's silly, really."

"Not if it's important to you, it isn't."

Still, she was reluctant to bring up the subject, knowing how idiotic it would sound. She was an adult, had made her choices in life, and crying about what could never be would merely show her as weak. The most important thing her father had taught her was to never show a weakness. To anyone, friend or foe. It could come back to hurt you someday.

"Let's talk about something else," she suggested.

Jake rolled onto his side to face her. Their eyes met, his shrouded in the darkness. "Something happened in there to upset you. Tell me what it was."

It wasn't a demand, it was an offer to listen. Did she really have anyone else she could talk to, besides Jake? What a terrible thought. After all these years of bottling all her emotions inside, she'd finally found someone willing to listen, no matter what she had to say.

"I've always wanted to be a kindergarten teacher."

"Then why didn't you?"

No condemnation at all. He didn't laugh at her or tell her it was a stupid idea. "Because I'm the last Fairchild."

"So?"

She turned on her side and rested her head in her hand. "Fairchilds have always worked for the firm."

"Kind of an antiquated way of thinking, isn't it?"

She sighed. "Yes and no. Fairchild Law is a family business. Founded by Fairchilds and headed by Fairchilds for generations before me. My father had no brothers or sisters, and I'm his only child. Which meant that if I didn't go into law, the family business would die out with my father."

He reached out and ran a finger over her cheek. She shivered and heated at the same time.

"I think your first responsibility should be to yourself. You deserve to be happy, Lucy. And if that means a different line of work, then you should go for it."

She shook her head. "It simply isn't done that way. I couldn't let my father down like that. He depends on me, depends on knowing that I'll be there to take over when he's no longer around."

"Does your father love you?"

"Of course he does."

"If he loved you then he'd want you to be happy."

She shifted onto her back again, unable to meet the challenging look in his eyes. "I am happy."

"Are you?"

"Yes."

"I don't think anyone can truly be happy living a lie."

Why had she allowed this conversation to continue? She knew it would lead to the inevitable self doubt that had plagued her for years. Torn between duty to family and dreams of a life of her own, she never managed to win the battle for herself, no matter how many different ways she played out the scenario in her mind.

She was doing the right thing. She was.

"That's one of the things I admire most about you," she said, turning the tables on him.

He tilted his head. "What's that?"

"You're the proverbial self-made man. Everything you have you worked for. You set a goal, and spent years pounding away at it until you reached it. You went from a homeless teenage runaway to a successful business owner. I admire you for that, Jake."

He didn't respond, instead stared at her as if struggling for a response.

"Nobody's ever said that to me before. Thanks."

"You're welcome."

Her gaze caught a shooting star whisking across the clear night sky, and for a brief second she closed her eyes and wished. Silly, she knew, but still, she made that never-to-be-granted wish.

After all, the night was for fantasy and dreams anyway. Why not wish on a dream just for fun?

"What did you wish for?" Jake whispered.

She turned to him and met his smile. "How do you

know I made a wish?"

"It's written all over your face. Besides, I saw the star and when I looked at you right afterward, your eyes were closed but your lips were moving."

"I see. And did you wish on the same star?"

"I asked you first." He grinned and swept her hair away from her face, his palm warm. Instead of pulling away, he left it resting on her neck. She felt her pulse pound rapidly against his hand.

"If I tell you my wish it won't come true."

He laughed. "That's what everyone says. I don't believe it."

"Do you want to risk telling me your wish?"

"Hmm, interesting dilemma."

"Why?"

"Because my wish was about you."

Her body quaked, but not from chill. His words were spoken in a low voice, husky with a sensual promise. She was almost afraid to ask him to reveal his wish, and too curious not to.

"Tell me."

"I wished that I could hold you in my arms and kiss you under the stars."

His words cut through her defenses and went straight to her heart. That he would wish for a kiss from her was unexpected, not to mention thrilling.

"That means I hold your destiny in my hands," she said, reveling in the heady feel of knowing Jake desired her.

"Yeah, you do. So?"

"So, what?" she teased.

"Does my wish come true or not?"

Without hesitation, she said, "Most definitely. Your wish is granted."

His expression turned dark as he loomed over her, not waiting more than a whispered breath to pull her against him and lower his mouth to hers.

Warm lips covered hers, coaxing a response that sounded more like a gasp than a pleasured sigh. And yet it was both. Jake held such barely leashed passion within that when he let it out it was near overwhelming, but not unwelcome. She eagerly pressed against him, sliding her arms around his shoulders and pulling him toward her. She wanted his body to cover hers, the same way his mouth had taken her lips.

"I waited all damn day for this," he said through clenched teeth. His hand slid up underneath the sweatshirt, under her tank top, fluttering along her rib cage on a relentless search. She knew he wouldn't be satisfied until he grasped what he sought.

His thumb found her nipple and flicked it gently. She gasped and arched into his hand as his palm covered her breast, gently squeezing and kneading the instantly aroused flesh.

Clouds had blown in and covered the moonlit sky, rendering them in darkness. Wind had blown out the candles he'd set, forcing them to rely on touch and sound rather than sight.

Lucy longed to see his face, and yet his voice, his breathing, his every touch told her all she needed to know. He was like a man on a mission, and his mission was her.

No part of her remained untouched. His hands wandered everywhere, from her breasts to her ribcage and over her hips. With a swift tug he pulled her shorts down and off, the now cool breeze biting against her bare legs before he threw the blankets over them again.

"Dammit, it's dark and I want to see you," he rasped in her ear. Heat burned through, his very words like a scorching fire that she knew she shouldn't touch but couldn't stay away from.

Somewhere in the back of her mind she considered suggesting they move into the house, where she could see him. She'd thought about him, about his body, from the first moment she'd laid eyes on him, her imagination conjuring up vivid images of a bronzed, god-like statue. Her most fervent wish was to see that statue unclothed before her, so she could admire and touch every angle and curve of his hardened body.

But her mind wouldn't cooperate. She didn't want to break the spell he'd woven over her, didn't want to take a chance that he would stop like he'd done before. This time she was stone cold sober and didn't want to stop. This time she wanted it all.

His lips against the pulse point on her throat set her on fire. He licked and nibbled her neck until she cried out a gasp that he covered with his mouth.

She could barely take the overwhelming sensations he evoked, and yet he was relentless. He simply would not stop. Not that she'd ask him to. But she refrained from begging for more.

His work-roughened hand slid over her hipbone and down her thigh, alternately clenching and unclenching as it squeezed her tender flesh.

She felt his erection pulsing hard against her hip as he leaned into her, and longed to wrap her fingers around that part of him. But he seemed to be eluding her questing hands.

"Jake, please. I want to touch you."

"Plenty of time for that later," he said in a rough voice, then gently parted her thighs with his hand and slid his palm against her aching sex.

Never before had sparks of pleasure flown through her with such intensity as they did the moment he touched her sensitive flesh. Instinctively she rocked against his palm, aiding his questing fingers by arching her hips.

She was already so close to orgasm she knew it was only a matter of seconds before she exploded against his hand. When he slipped his fingers under her silk panties and parted her slick folds, she bit her lip to keep from crying out her pleasure.

Gently, he eased one, then two fingers inside her, boldly praising her aroused state. She couldn't have said two words if her life depended on it. All she could do was gasp, and pray fervently that he rode out this storm with her, that he didn't pull away as he'd done before.

Mindless with passion, she heard only his murmuring in her ear, coaxing her to let go, each spoken word coupled with the agonizing pleasure of his fingers moving within her, his thumb circling the sensitive nub.

Finally the moment was upon her, and she held on to his shoulders and pushed against his hand, her buttocks rising up as he drove her over the edge, taking in her cries of pleasure with his lips as he kissed her through her shuddering climax.

He held her, kissing her as she gradually regained some semblance of sanity. He pulled her against him and laid her head on his shoulder, one of her legs flung over his, just as she'd wished earlier. He didn't say a word, just stroked her back while her breathing returned to normal.

What could she say to him after what had just happened? She'd never lost control like that before. She'd never had a sexual experience like that before, never had a man put her pleasure before his own.

But now that he'd shown her how unselfish he was, how giving, she wanted to return the favor. Boldly she reached out her hand and caressed his chest, curling her fingers in the crisp hairs above his shirt.

"Now, it's your turn." She smiled into the darkness as he sucked in a breath.

Something cold and wet hit her forehead. Once, twice, then several more.

"It's raining." Jake jumped up in a flash as the sky

opened, drenching them in a downpour. He motioned for Lucy to hurry, which she did as best she could, struggling with the last vestiges of her modesty as she scurried back into her clothes and grabbed what blankets she could hold. Jake jumped off the trampoline and held his arms out to her. She leaned into him and he swept her onto the ground. They both took off in a brisk run toward the house.

Rascal was inside the door, wagging his tail for them.

Once inside, Jake grabbed the now-soaked blankets and laid them in another room, returning with a towel for her.

She dried her wet skin and hair, not once taking her eyes off the man who, moments ago, had taken her to a height of pleasure that still left her shaking and wanting more.

"I can't believe it's raining like that." His eyes darkened to a smoldering amber.

Lucy felt the stirrings of arousal surround her once again, knowing the magic of this night was just beginning. "Maybe it was a sign that it was time to come inside."

He nodded, then stepped toward her, gathering her in his arms. Their eyes met and held, and she felt every blissful second tick by as he lowered his face to hers.

Then her cell phone rang.

Jake lifted his head.

"Ignore it," she said.

He nodded and the phone stopped ringing. "Now,

where were we?"

The phone rang again.

Lucy sighed. "I'd better check to see who that is."

He pulled away while she ran to the dining room to retrieve her telephone. Seeing the home number, she answered.

"Lucille?"

It was her father. She knew she shouldn't have answered. When would she learn to listen to that voice inside her head? "Yes?"

"I need you to come home."

She sighed. "Father, really. I thought we had this discussion before. I'm old enough to—"

"You don't understand," he interrupted. "I'm having chest pains. I thought it was indigestion but they won't go away. In fact, they're getting worse."

Panic flew through her, and she began to shake. "Father, call 911 now!"

"No, it's not that bad. I just don't want to be here alone in case something happens."

Knowing how stubborn her father could be about medical issues, she said, "I'll be there as soon as I can."

She hung up and turned to Jake, who had come into the room and was standing behind her.

"Jake, I'm sorry, I have to go. My father is having chest pains and he's so stubborn and won't go to the doctor and—"

Jake took a step and gathered her in his arms,

placing a kiss on the top of her head. "Hey, it's okay. Go, take care of your dad."

She wished she could bring him along, felt a desperate need for his strength. But she knew she couldn't because his presence would only make things worse. "I'm sorry. Jake, I'm so sorry," she said at the same time gathering her purse and slipping on her sandals.

"We'll have more nights like tonight. Go, and be careful."

Pressing a quick kiss to his lips she flew out the door toward her car, hoping her father merely had another attack of indigestion.

He may be an insufferable pain in the butt, but he was the only family she had. Once inside the vehicle, she quickly started it up, counting the minutes until she'd reach home.

Chapter Nine

Lucy wrapped her arms around herself and paced the library, trying her best not to glare at her father.

He was fine. There was nothing wrong with him. High color fused his face. He wasn't even pale. No sweating, his pulse was strong. He looked fit and robust as he sat reading the financial section of the paper while she paced and fumed.

Oh, he'd tried to give her his best oh-poor-pitiful-me performance when she'd flown through the front door and raced to his side after breaking nearly every speed record between Jake's house and hers, frantic and praying that she wouldn't find her father passed out on the floor when she got there...or worse.

He'd been sitting in that very chair, slumped, but rosy cheeked, looking up at her with his sad, puppy dog eyes. He'd coughed, raised a limp hand up to her. Then she'd known. Her father would never go down easy. He'd fight his own death...to the death.

"How do you feel now?" she asked through gritted teeth.

"A little better. The aspirin helped, I think. Thank

you."

His voice was faint, barely above a whisper. The man was never going to win an Academy Award for his performance. Honestly, he really was a pathetic liar. He was a master at manipulation in the courtroom, but she knew him all too well. She saw right through this act for exactly what it was—a way to separate her from Jake. Somehow he'd known she was with Jake and he'd had to pull this dying act to get her to come home. Though a part of her wasn't one hundred percent certain that was true, so here she was, playing nursemaid for what she was almost sure was no good reason.

"It means so much to me to have you here by my side, Lucille. I don't know what I would have done if you hadn't been here."

Fumed that his ploy hadn't worked, no doubt. Then strategized a full blown stroke. Or set the house on fire. "You have a house full of servants, Father."

He shook his head, raising his hand in a weak attempt to brush it through his hair. "It's not the same thing. You're the only family I have. If something had happened and I would have...passed on without seeing you..."

She turned away and rolled her eyes, then sat with her father for another hour while he read the financials. She watched the clock until he finally decided to go to bed, then she said she was going to bed, too. She went up to her room, closed the door, and waited another hour, even creeping over to her father's wing of the house to make certain his light was off.

It was only ten. She was irritated, pent up and angry at her father for ruining what would have been a very special evening with Jake. She picked up her cell phone and hesitated only a few seconds before pressing the button. Jake answered on the first ring.

"How's your dad?"

She smiled. "He's fine. False alarm."

She heard him exhale. "That's great news."

"I think he faked it to get me home."

Jake paused. "Seriously?"

"Yes. I can't be sure, but I have my suspicions." She waited, a bit nervous about inviting herself back over there. It was a Saturday, and he might have plans for the next day.

"So, can you sneak out without Daddy catching you?"

She giggled, feeling like a teenager. "Yes, I think so. Are you sure you want me to come back?"

"We need to finish what we started. Don't get a ticket speeding over here, but hurry the hell up."

She hung up, feeling a thrill of excitement and warmth as she changed clothes, brushed her teeth and tiptoed out the back door toward the garage. The thirty-minute drive to Jake's house seemed like hours. Thankfully, the rain had stopped, leaving a glassy sheen on the roads. But that also meant she had to slow down. It didn't stop her pulse from racing, though.

By the time she pulled into his driveway, her heart

was jackhammering and her palms were sweaty. He opened the front door before she'd even started up the walk. She held her breath at the sight of him leaning against the doorway, an open bottle of beer in his hand and a half-smile on his face. God, he was so sexy. And he was hers.

For tonight, anyway.

"Took you long enough."

"I was trying not to get a ticket since I practically broke the land speed record on the way home."

He moved out of the way to let her inside, then shut and locked the front door, leading the way into the living room. "Sorry he put you through that."

Lucy sat on the sofa, kicked off her sandals and ran both hands through her unruly hair. "I'm used to it."

Jake arched a brow. "He has fake heart attacks a lot?"

"No. He manipulates me to get his own way." She shifted to face him. "But I couldn't take the chance that something might be seriously wrong with him."

"I understand. You're a good daughter."

She shrugged. "He's in bed now. He's fine. And I'm here, with you."

"Yeah, you are. Thanks for coming back."

"Thanks for letting me."

Lucy suddenly felt awkward, which made her even angrier at her father. Things between her and Jake had been perfect earlier. He had taken her to a magical place. There had been heat and passion brewing between them, and with one phone call her father had put this invisible wedge between her and Jake that she wasn't sure how to remove.

"Stop thinking."

"What?" she asked.

"You're still angry at your dad. He's interfering. Push him out the door."

Jake was right. Her father was still winning. She refused to let that happen. She pulled her legs up on the sofa and leaned into Jake. "Then kiss me until I can't think anymore."

Apparently he didn't need to be asked twice, because he dragged her into his arms and kissed her. Deep, and with the same mind-boggling passion he'd shown her outside earlier. In a matter of minutes Lucy was fully involved in Jake, all thoughts of her father scattering away.

Now all she knew was Jake's mouth, the way he moved it over hers in a soft but insistent way. The way he coaxed her lips to part, sliding his tongue inside so she could sample the tangy flavor of beer that still lingered there. He pulled her onto his lap and his hands dove under the sweatshirt, warm and palming the skin of her stomach. She melted into his embrace, settling against him as he widened his legs.

His erection pushed against her hip and the fact that he could be turned on—by her—was a heady, exhilarating experience. It gave her a sense of power, of feeling equal to him because he sure hit her hot buttons in a major way.

He lifted his head. “I’m glad you came back. I’ve been thinking about you since you left.”

“You have?”

“Yeah. I can still smell you, can still taste you, and if you didn’t come back tonight I might have had to sneak into your house and up to your bedroom.”

She thrilled at the thought of it. Jake in her room. “And what would you have done when you got there?”

“Hopefully made you scream loud enough to bring your father running.” His fingers splayed along the bare expanse of her lower belly, under the waistband of her shorts. He cupped her sex and she was instantly transported to earlier tonight, to how his touch had skyrocketed her into a blinding orgasm. She wanted that again, only this time, she wanted him to go with her.

She lifted against his hand, and whispered his name on a breathless moan.

“Let’s go stretch out on my bed before I lose control again.” He lifted her off his lap and set her on her feet, then took her by the hand.

He’d lost control before? She was pretty certain it had been her who’d totally lost her mind outside. But she liked that he thought himself out of control. She also liked the fact that he held her hand as they walked down the hall, that he seemed to be connected to her emotionally, beyond just this physical act they were about to engage in.

When they entered the bedroom he flipped on the light. “Sorry, it’s a little messy and not fancy.”

She barely remembered his room from the other night, when she'd passed out in a drunken stupor, then woken up hazy and disoriented.

His room had a double bed, with a nice brown quilt that looked handmade. Two simple end tables on each side, a dresser and chest of drawers and a couple lamps. Typical guy room. But she liked that he wasn't overly fussy. "It's a nice room, Jake. Who made the quilt?"

He scratched his nose and looked across at the bed, not at her. "My, uh, my grandmother."

Oh, how sweet. "I love it. It's beautiful." She moved to the side of the bed and began to fold the quilt down to the foot of the bed. Jake went to the other side and helped her. A simple task, yet it felt domestic. Intimate. Nothing like the GQ guys who had made it such a seduction scene when she'd had sex before. Their bedrooms had set the scene so perfectly, as if they'd done it hundreds of times before. It had left her cold. This was so different, so perfect. She smiled at Jake across the bed. He came over to her side and lifted her in his arms.

"Enough small talk. I want to make love to you."

She gasped, then laughed when he pushed her onto the bed. Her smile died when he crawled onto the bed and lay on top of her, framing her face with his hands. His pelvis aligned with hers, the ridge of his hard shaft insistent as he swept his lips over hers. There was something monumental and heady about him kissing her, and his body's reaction to that. Not to mention her own body's wild reaction.

Her heart jacked up its rhythm to near crazy speed. She had to calm down or she'd end up passing out. Again. That would be really bad. Tonight she intended to be calm and clear headed. Or at least clear headed. She was pretty certain calm was going to be out of the question, especially with Jake's questing fingers doing incredible things to her stomach on their way up to her breasts. When he skimmed across her nipples, calm shredded and she arched against his fingers. He made her feel wild, made her want things she hadn't wanted in...well, she'd never really craved sex before. Now she did, and it was the most decadent feeling to really want a man like she wanted Jake, to have all these feelings inside just bursting to get out.

He slid his fingers under her bra and found her nipple. The way he watched her while he touched her was unnerving, and yet so hot, so incredibly erotic she felt like she'd combust all over. She wanted more, so much more, and she shifted to her side so she could touch him, too. She rolled his shirt up over his stomach, her fingers curling into the hard planes of his flesh and the soft down she found there. So much to see, so much to touch. She wanted hours—days—to explore him, to see him. Thank God he'd left the light on. She loved seeing his face, his body, his hands on her.

He pushed her over onto her back again, and she started to protest, but then he lifted her sweatshirt and tank top off, and she understood. It was time to get naked, and she was all for that. Anything that would speed up the process of getting skin to skin. She leaned up on her elbows and watched him take his shirt off, admired the hard planes of his stomach, his tanned chest and well defined arms, as he leaned over her and pulled the straps of her bra down, kissing her shoulder, her collarbone, and the swell of her breast. She sighed in absolute wonder that he'd take his time with her. The men she'd been with before had been after the big payoff—foreplay hadn't really been their thing.

Then again, the men she'd been with before had been nothing like Jake.

He unhooked her bra and removed it, then bent and captured her nipple between his lips. When he flicked his tongue over the bud, she tilted her head back and gasped, lost in the sensation, the wet heat, the wonder of finally being right where she wanted to be.

Jake made quick work of her shorts and panties, then his own shorts.

Finally, both of them naked, she sat up and looked her fill of him. She'd waited a long time for this, had thought about it nonstop since she first met him.

He didn't disappoint. He was kneeling, his legs slightly apart, and she was in awe.

Someone should sculpt the man. He wasn't perfect—there were scars here and there—his arms, one on his chest, a few on his legs. The funny thing was, that only added to the pure maleness of him. He was so...real. His body wasn't one created in the gym. It was honed from daily, backbreaking work, and it showed. All that beautiful muscle, and she couldn't resist skimming her palms over his chest, down his stomach, his hips. Her gaze lifted to his. He watched her as she touched him, but he hadn't said a word. His eyes said it all—such male approval in the intensity of his gaze. She fisted his cock—so hot, so utterly primal. He hissed, the sound shooting right to her core. She grew wet and anxious and needy just touching this part of him, stroking him, feeling him surge against her hand in silent demand for more. She knew right then that what was going to happen between them was going to be incredible.

He threaded his fingers through her hair and brought her face to his, his lips covering hers, his tongue entering her mouth with such depth, such passion, that it stole her breath. And still, she held on to him, continuing to squeeze and stroke him, feeling the weight and heat of him in her hand until he grasped her wrist and pulled her hand away, pushing her body down on the bed and covering it with his.

His cock surged between her legs, teasing her sex until she shuddered with the need to feel him inside her. His kisses, the way his hands roamed over her body, tortured her, made her need their joining with desperation.

And still, all he did was kiss her, move against her, palm her sex with his hand and caress her in easy, gentle strokes that stoked the fire inside her to an inferno. She was going to climax—for the second time tonight—and Jake hadn't even had his first one yet. But she couldn't stop it, not the way he possessed her with masterful strokes, easy and yet demanding, taking her ever higher until she had no hope to maintain control. She burst into a fiery orgasm, arching against his hand and whimpering as she rode the flames he stoked, holding tight to Jake until she collapsed.

He stroked her breasts and belly until she turned to him and smiled, then he kissed her, cupped her sex, and began again, sliding his fingers inside her and bringing her desire up full force yet again. She tore her lips from his and searched his face.

"Jake, please."

His jaw was set tight as he looked down at her. But she knew it wasn't anger in his expression—it was the same gripping need she felt. He rolled over and opened the drawer on his night stand and pulled out a condom, tore open the package and put it on, then parted her thighs as he moved between them. He slipped one hand underneath her, raising her butt, and settled on top of her, sliding his tongue along her bottom lip, then kissing her with a feather light touch that made her shudder.

He slid inside her, slow and easy, his gaze glued to hers as he did. It was such a powerful, emotional moment. She knew she was making too much of it, that it was just sex and nothing more. But this whole night had been so different than any other for her, she couldn't help it. Jake was special, and despite the internal warning in her head to keep her heart intact, as soon as he scooped her up and held her tight and started moving against her, it was so sweet and so tender, her heart just lost it. She was invested and she knew she was hopelessly in love with him.

He shifted, flexed his fingers against her hip and surged, giving her more. She dug her heels into the mattress and arched against him, meeting his every thrust. He stroked her breasts, her neck, kissing her with such depth it moved her to tears. Lucy took it all in with wonder and excitement, exploring everything—the way he possessed her, the look on his face, the way he made her feel—special and loved. And maybe she was making all this up. Maybe Jake didn't really feel that way about her. But right now, she was the only woman in the world to him, and nothing else mattered. It was the two of them, every other care and concern shut out. He was focused only on her, and she on him.

And when Jake began to increase the pace, shifting so he held tight to her, pushed harder, faster, she was along for the ride, right there with him, tightening inside and close to orgasm. He slid both hands underneath her buttocks to lift her, then buried himself deep inside her. The intimacy unraveled her, and when he pressed his lips to hers, sliding his tongue between them to lick at hers with the softest, velvety strokes that tingled all over, she shattered, her orgasm bursting throughout her body. Jake thrust once more and shuddered against her, burying his face in her neck, licking the column of her throat and sending shivers along her skin to couple with the lightning sensations already devastating her senses.

She floated back to reality like a falling leaf on a no wind day—easy, gently. Jake stroked her sweat-soaked body in slow, measured movements, from her collarbone to her neck to her hips, still moving inside her.

"Mmmm," was all she could manage.

Jake rolled to the side, bringing her with him. She loved looking at him, the way his eyes had this satisfied, kind of glazed-over look. Did she look the same way? She hoped so.

He let his fingers roam over her hip, gently squeezing, and still he moved against her, her body coming to life once again. She raised her leg over his hip and rocked against him. Jake's lips curled. "I never took you for insatiable."

"Do you know how long it's been?"

"No. Tell me."

"I don't have sex often. Hardly ever, actually." She probably shouldn't tell him that. Too late now.

"So you're making up for lost time?"

She nodded. "Yes. I hope you're up for it. I might be on a roll now."

Jake arched a brow, then withdrew from her only long enough to dispose of the condom and reach for the box in the bedside drawer. "Good thing I'm well prepared."

She laughed, loving that she could be herself with him. She reached into the box and took out a packet, handing it to him with a smile. "Good thing."

He grabbed the packet in his hand, then gathered her in his arms. "I have a feeling neither of us is going to get any sleep tonight."

As Jake took her mouth in a deep, lingering kiss, Lucy had a feeling neither of them was going to complain about the lack of sleep.

Chapter Ten

Lucy stood at the door to Jake's trailer a little before noon on Monday, her heart pounding in excitement and trepidation. She had a bag of sandwiches and thought she'd surprise him by bringing him lunch. A little presumptuous on her part, but after spending the weekend with him, she was pretty certain things between them had changed. Still, maybe she should have called first.

You're being ridiculous. He'll be happy to see you. Just knock.

She did, and cringed when his curt "What?" followed. Maybe she should just turn around and hightail it out of there. No, that would be stupid. She'd walked all the way over here from her office. She was going to suck it up and tell him she was here. He would be happy to see her, she knew it.

"Jake, it's Lucy."

He jerked the door open, and her smile died. Maybe it wasn't a good day for lunch after all.

"Did I come at a bad time?"

"No. Come in. Sorry."

He held the door open while she climbed the stairs up and into the trailer.

"Am I interrupting?" She smoothed loose tendrils of hair back from her face, then took a quick glance at his desk. Papers and blueprints were spread out everywhere, and lots of other paperwork—crumpled up and tossed—littered the floor of the trailer.

"No. I'm just dealing with some...stuff today."

"Bad stuff?"

"I don't want to talk about it."

Obviously. "I brought lunch." She tried again for a smile.

"Uh, I already ate."

Again, her smile died. "Oh. I'm sorry. I should have called first. I just thought you might enjoy a little break."

"Like I said. It's a bad day, Lucy. I don't have much time for a break."

Heat rose up her neck and cheeks. She snatched up the lunch bag and crushed it between her hands. "I'm really sorry, Jake. I should have called. I just assumed..."

"Well, call next time, okay?"

Oh, God. This hurt. It was like being dismissed by her father all over again. That taciturn look of disapproval, like she was bothering him when all she wanted was a little attention.

You are so needy, Lucille Fairchild. When are you going to get over that?

Never.

The throb of hurt swelled through her body. She wanted to crumple right there, but she couldn't, refused to do it. She'd never let Jake see that he'd hurt her. It was such a silly thing, really. He'd never understand. It wasn't his fault. It was hers.

Tears welled and she had to get out of there before she made an utter fool of herself. "Of course. I only had a few minutes, anyway. I need to go."

"Lucy..."

"No, really." She already had the door open. "I'll talk to you later, Jake." Just a few steps down and she could make her escape.

"Lucy, wait."

Please, please don't follow me. She felt stupid already. She pulled the door shut behind her and nearly flew down the stairs, grateful she'd worn a pantsuit and flats today. She made quick time across the gravel yard and onto the sidewalk, hurrying back to the office. Thankfully it was the lunch hour and no one was about. She tucked herself into her office and shut the door, leaving a message for her secretary that she didn't want to take any calls for the rest of the afternoon. She pulled off her jacket and fell into her chair, tossing the lunch bag on her desk with a grimace.

She grabbed a tissue and wiped away her foolish tears, then leaned back in her chair.

Stupid idea, anyway. What was she thinking? That one weekend of sex and she and Jake were now a couple?

That she could just show up on his jobsite and interrupt his day? He was busy. Just like she was. Instead of mooning over her all day long, Jake was actually doing his job. Which was exactly what she should have been doing today. Instead, she'd spent the morning thinking about Jake, about their weekend, about the time they'd spent in bed together.

Ugh. She was such a...woman.

Damn estrogen anyway.

They weren't a couple. They weren't even dating, for God's sake. She'd helped him out with his party. They had chemistry together, so they'd made a mutually agreeable decision and had sex. They were both mature, consenting adults who could do what they want. There was no commitment, no relationship.

They had nothing together.

And she thought she was in love with Jake.

She had to grow up, had to stop living out this fantasy where she could find the perfect guy who would swoop in and take all the hurt away.

That kind of guy didn't exist. Not in her world. Maybe he didn't exist at all.

She really needed to get out more. She'd already invested too much of her heart in a man who clearly didn't want the same things.

It was time for her to move on, before she really got hurt.

She spent the rest of the day deeply involved in work

projects, which helped to rid her mind of anything and everything having to do with Jake. By the time she got home that night, she felt immensely better.

That is, until she'd changed clothes and went in search of her father, hoping spending the evening with him would be a nice distraction.

She found her father in the library.

With Alex.

Ugh. As if the day hadn't already been a disaster. She plastered on a polite smile and walked in.

"Alex."

"Lucy. You look lovely, as usual."

"Thank you. What a...surprise to see you here." She couldn't bring herself to call it a nice surprise.

"I had a case to go over with your father, and he kindly invited me over for cocktails."

"I see." She smelled setup. She slanted a glance at her father, who beamed a smile like he was the father of the bride and today was her wedding day.

In your dreams, Daddy.

"We were just finishing up, Lucille," her father said. "I was hoping you'd come home in time."

Lucy arched a brow. "In time for what?"

"To go out to dinner with me," Alex said.

Setup. She knew it. "I'm exhausted, Alex. It's been a really long day."

Alex took her hand and slid it in the crook of his arm. "Nonsense. A nice quiet dinner at an out-of-the-way place, a glass of wine to relax you, and I'll have you home in a couple hours. It's only seven thirty."

Dammit. Why couldn't she be bitchy and just tell him she didn't like him, that she'd rather eat dinner with the servants than share a meal at a fancy restaurant with him? The servants were better company, and infinitely more fun to talk to.

Because she was terrible at saying no. And her father knew it, because he had that knowing smile on his face that said he'd already won.

Besides, what else would she do tonight? Eat with her father, who would no doubt lecture her? Or she could spend the evening in her room moping about Jake and feeling sorry for herself.

At least spending a couple hours with Alex would take her mind off her own problems. Alex was famous for talking about himself. He'd keep her thoughts occupied by steering the conversation around to all things Alex. And she'd be utterly bored to exhaustion and could then come home and fall into a coma.

Perfect.

"Uh, sure. Why not? But we have to make an early evening of it. I have to be in court first thing in the morning."

"Of course." Alex was already leading her toward the door. "Good night, Ray."

"Good night, Alex, Lucille. You two have fun and don't worry about staying out too late. I'll be fine here."

Oh, sure. He was *fine* when she went out with Alex,

but near dying whenever she was with Jake. Honestly. The man was as transparent as tape.

Alex drove them into the city, to one of the newer restaurants serving California food, which meant high-priced meals, very little food on the plate. Lucy would have preferred a cheeseburger. Or maybe barbecue.

Don't think of Jake. Though it was difficult not to, considering Alex droned on and on with talk of himself, his job, his successes, his new car, the house he was buying.

He ordered the very best wine on the menu, the highest-priced food, then presumed to order her dinner like she was some blithering idiot who couldn't read the menu and decide for herself. Before she could complain about that, he launched into the case he'd won today as if he were the best attorney in the city. He never bothered to ask about her day, her week, her month, anything about her life or how she was doing.

Did everything have to be about him? He could be at the table by himself—or with anyone, frankly—and it wouldn't matter. The man was completely narcissistic and a pretentious snob. She had nothing in common with him, and the thought of ever marrying a man like Alex nauseated her.

Being with Alex made her miserable.

Surely somewhere out there was the right guy for her.

No, that wasn't quite right. She had already met the right guy for her. Sitting here having to endure this miserable night with Alex cemented that fact.

She missed Jake. Jake was the right guy for her, dammit.

Where had she gone wrong? It sucked when you cared about someone and they didn't return your feelings.

She counted the hours until this farce of an evening with Alex was over. Tomorrow, she was going to make an attempt to talk to Jake again. She was an attorney, a fighter. A Fairchild never gave up that easy, especially when it really counted.

She hadn't been mistaken about her feelings for Jake. Or about his feelings for her. So he'd had a bad day. She'd made too much of his mood and let her own feelings of inadequacy guide her.

She wasn't ready to give up yet.

Jake pulled up in front of Lucy's house, knowing this wasn't going to be easy. She was either going to answer the door, and he was going to have to explain his behavior earlier today, or her father was going to answer the door.

Neither situation was going to be pleasant.

He walked up and rang the doorbell. Time to man up and face the consequences. He'd acted like an ass earlier today. Worse than an ass. So he had a million things on his mind, so several things hadn't gone his way. So he'd been in a bad mood.

His lady had showed up with lunch. He should have dropped everything and paid attention to her. He should have had the decency to at least be grateful.

Instead, he'd been surly, ungracious, and all but slammed the door in her face.

What the hell had been wrong with him, anyway?

Fear, that's what it was. She'd showed up at his trailer, beautiful, smiling, and the first thing he thought was...she was his.

He wanted Lucy in his life, and not just today. He could see having lunch with her every damn day for the rest of his life. And breakfast. And dinner.

Frankly, that had scared the hell out of him.

Yeah, he'd had a bad morning, but that didn't excuse his actions. He'd deliberately pushed her away because she scared him. His feelings for her scared him. She'd acted like a woman in love, and she'd scared the shit out of him. So he'd behaved like an asshole.

She should slam the door right in his face. He'd been so rude to her today. It was unforgiveable.

Unfortunately, Lucy didn't open the front door. Raymond Fairchild arched a brow and offered up a distasteful expression.

"Mr. Dalton."

"Mr. Fairchild. Is Lucy home?"

"As a matter of fact, she is not. She's out for the evening with her fiancé."

"Excuse me?"

"She went out with Alex tonight."

Not this again. "They're not engaged."

"I beg to differ, Mr. Dalton. She might have dallied

with you, but Lucille has since come to her senses and has agreed to marry Alex Sheldon. They're off right now planning their wedding."

Jake crossed his arms. He didn't believe Raymond Fairchild for one minute. "Uh huh. Just tell Lucy I came by."

Waste of time. Her father wouldn't deliver the message. Jake knew that. "On second thought, never mind. I'll call her tomorrow."

Fairchild just smiled, his grin slimy as a snake's. "They're at La Chateau on Market Street if you'd like to check it out for yourself. Good night, Mr. Dalton."

Lucy's father closed the door. Jake turned on his heel and went back to his truck, having no intention of checking out the restaurant where Lucy was allegedly having dinner with Alex. But he found himself jumping on the freeway and doing just that, pulling into an empty spot on the street right in front of the restaurant. Trendy, modern, with glass windows that showed everything going on inside.

As luck would have it, he spotted Lucy and Alex with the best seat in the house, right next to the front window. Drinking wine and having dinner. Smiling. Talking together. They made a nice couple. Jake's stomach tightened.

Alex picked up Lucy's hand and pressed his lips to it. Lucy's lips parted, her eyes wide. With pleasure, maybe?

Jake didn't need to see more than that. He pulled away from the curb, realizing he'd been all wrong about

Lucy. He might have thrown her out of his trailer today, but it didn't take her long to run back into Alex's arms.

Hell, maybe that's why she'd brought him lunch today—to sit down and break things off with him. Publicly, at his place of work so he wouldn't cause a scene.

Yeah, he was an idiot. Just because you slept with a woman didn't mean she cared about you. Just because you might be falling in love with her didn't mean she returned your feelings.

He had a lot of things to learn about the rich folk.

He should have never taken that walk on the other side of the tracks. He knew where he belonged.

From now on, he'd stay there.

The three hours Lucy had spent in Alex's company were the longest in her entire life. When he'd picked up her hand and kissed it at the restaurant, she thought she might lose her dinner. Really, his attempts at seduction were revolting and something out of a nonfiction book on how to seduce women—blatantly obvious.

She'd sat there, utterly appalled for a few seconds while he pressed his mouth to her hand, then slid his tongue out—yes, he actually licked her. Ew. Shocked, she'd been momentarily stunned and unable to move or utter a word, afraid she'd either scream at him or burst out laughing. She'd finally recovered enough to jerk her hand away and wipe the back of it with the napkin in her lap. When he'd followed up with his best attempt at a smoldering, seductive look, she'd snorted and masked it by faking a cough.

The rest of the evening had pretty much gone downhill. Alex had reiterated what a great "match" they'd make together, using words like "partnership" and "merger" until she finally rolled her eyes and told him point blank that she wasn't the least bit interested in him, romantically or otherwise. Then she'd stared out her window the entire ride home, refusing to let Alex walk her to the door. She'd practically run to her front door and hurried inside, locked the deadbolt behind her and peeked out the peephole to be certain Alex wouldn't try to come inside.

Hopefully she'd made her feelings more than clear to him.

"Where's Alex?"

Lucy jumped and let out a squeal at her father's voice right behind her. She pivoted and placed her hands on her hips.

"Good Lord, Father. You scared me. Quit lurking."

"I wanted to see how your date went."

She brushed past him and went into the library, sliding onto one of the leather chairs so she could kick off her shoes. "It wasn't a date. And it was horrible. Alex is a pompous moron. Spending any time alone with him is torture. I don't like him, have nothing in common with him, and if you try to foist him on me again I'll move out. Is that clear?"

Her father glared at her. "Really, Lucille. You've hardly

given Alex a chance."

Lucy sighed and leaned forward, wishing she could make her father see reality. "I don't have feelings for Alex."

Raymond snorted. "What do feelings have to do with anything? You two are a good match on paper."

She rolled her eyes. "I want someone to love, Father. How difficult is that to comprehend?"

"Love means you're not thinking with your head. Who do you want, Lucille? That rough construction worker Jake Dalton?"

Yes. "I want someone to love me. I want a relationship based on emotions, not balance sheets."

"Love is messy."

"Love is perfect." It was like talking to the wall. He'd never understand.

"He was here tonight, you know."

Lucy's head shot up. "Who was here tonight? Jake?"

"Yes. I set him straight though."

Dread dropped her stomach to her feet. She gripped the edge of the chair. "What did you do?"

"I told him you had finally come to your senses and decided to marry Alex, of course. Which is what I thought was going to happen tonight."

She sank back into the chair. "Oh, Father. How could you do that? I'm not at all interested in Alex."

Her father tsked. She really hated when he did that.

"I only want what's best for you, Lucille."

Anger made her shoot to her feet. “No, you want what’s best for *you*. You aren’t thinking of me at all. You never do. You don’t care about me and what I want. You don’t think about me being happy. You think about the firm. You always have.”

“You’re being ridiculous, Lucille.”

“Am I? When did you become so heartless? Was it after Mother died, or have you always been this way?”

Anger mottled her father’s face. “Do not speak to me that way. Who is it that you think you want? That lowlife Jake Dalton?”

“He isn’t a lowlife. He’s built a solid business from the ground up. He works hard and he’s successful.”

“He’s not at all the type of man for you. He’s beneath you...beneath us. You could do much better.”

Disdain dripped off her father’s words. And prejudice. Maybe she’d avoided seeing it all these years, but there it was, plain as day.

“You’re a snob, Daddy. You don’t even know Jake. You haven’t even given him a chance.”

Her father lifted his chin. “Nor do I intend to. It would be a waste of my time. Just as he’s a waste of yours.”

Tears threatened, and she hated that. Having any further conversation with her father would be useless. She knew she needed to leave before she said something irreparable, something that would tear the fabric of her relationship with her father. She turned and fled from the room and went to her own wing, shutting and locking the door. She threw herself on her bed, feeling like the princess locked in the tower.

Okay, maybe she was being melodramatic, but her father's interference had to stop. Jake had been right when he'd told her she was too old to be living with her father. She hadn't counted on him manipulating her life to this extent.

She had to talk to Jake, to set things straight between them, let him know that her father had been wrong about her and Alex. It was time to change a few things about her living situation, about her life with her father.

It was time to stand on her own.

The next day she knew better than to try and see Jake at the construction site. No way was she going to risk having the door slammed in her face again. She could only imagine what must be going through his head, what he must have thought after his conversation with her father last night.

She'd avoided her father the entire day at work. Fortunately, spending the morning in court helped. After she went to lunch, she spent the remainder of the day locked up in meetings with a few of the junior attorneys going over pending casework. By the time the day ended, she had managed to successfully dodge her father. She raced home, changed clothes and was out the door before her father came home from the office.

Now she just had to convince Jake to see her. She pulled in his driveway, relieved to see his truck parked there and his garage door open. She heard the sound of mowing in the backyard and went through the gate, petting Rascal who bounded up to greet her. Rascal led her to Jake, who was just finishing up his lawn work. He turned when he saw her, and frowned.

Shirtless, covered in grass, sweat and dirt, he looked magnificent.

"What are you doing here?" He brushed past her to push the lawn mower toward the front of the house.

She followed, watching as he grabbed a towel and wiped his face. Yeah, still grimy. Still gorgeous. "I…I came to talk to you about last night."

Ignoring her, he turned on the hose and began to wash down the mower. "There's nothing more to talk about. Your father set things straight."

Undaunted, she stepped closer so he could hear her over the powerful noise of the water stream. "And who are you going to believe, Jake? Me or my father?"

"I saw you at the restaurant with Alex."

How nice of her father to tell Jake where she and Alex had been having dinner. "Yes, I went out to dinner with Alex."

Jake turned off the faucet and turned to her, then looked around the neighborhood. Other homeowners were washing cars or doing their own lawn work. "Let's take this inside."

She nodded and followed him through the garage and into the house. Jake stopped in the kitchen to grab two beers, opened both and handed her one. He leaned against the counter while she took a seat at the kitchen table.

"I went to dinner with Alex. He was at the house when I got home last night. I was...admittedly a bit hurt about lunch yesterday."

"So you decided to dump me and go back to Alex just because I couldn't have lunch with you?"

"No." She sighed, feeling like neither of them were seeing things clearly. "My father, and Alex, can be rather insistent."

"I hardly see you as a pushover, Lucy."

"You're right. It was stupid. I feel nothing for Alex and should have said no. I felt manipulated and cornered and I shouldn't have gone with him. But I did. And I had a miserable time. Alex droned on and on about himself and his life and I couldn't wait for dinner to be over."

"I saw him kiss your hand."

"I almost lost my dinner over it. I was so shocked when he did that it took me a full minute to register what he was doing. I jerked my hand away as soon as I could recover."

"Uh huh."

Really, the man's jealousy was exasperating. And kind of thrilling, too. "I made him take me home right after that. And when my father told me you had come by, and what he'd told you, I was furious with him."

"Yeah, I'll bet that hurt his feelings."

She rolled her eyes. "Look, Jake. I can't keep apologizing for my father. Only for myself. I'm sorry for barging in on you at lunch yesterday. I'm sorry I went out to dinner with Alex. Both were bad moves on my part. But I can't apologize anymore for my father. He's part of me. He's part of my life and my career. If you and I are going to have a relationship—"

"Is that what you think we have, Lucy? A relationship?"

Stunned, she didn't know how to answer that. "I don't know. I thought we were starting one. Was I wrong?"

He stared at her for so long she shifted in her chair, growing uncomfortable. She laid the beer on the table and stood. "Maybe I shouldn't have come."

"Wait."

He moved toward her, his chest still glistening with perspiration. She sucked in a breath and held it as he stopped in front of her.

She didn't want to lose him. She didn't want to hear him say goodbye to her.

"I'm sorry, Lucy. I'm a bad-tempered sonofabitch sometimes. And jealous as hell."

That's exactly what she wanted to hear.

"It's okay. I make a lot of wrong decisions, and I'm often blind to my father's faults. I always have been. I let him manipulate me all too often and I've got to learn to stop letting him do that to me. I guess I keep hoping he'll change. He doesn't."

He moved in even closer. "I was rude to you yesterday when you were nice enough to bring me lunch. I'm really sorry about that."

She shrugged. "It's okay. I should have called. I shouldn't assume..."

He reached for her, grasping her upper arms. "Yeah, you *should* assume. If we're going to have a relationship, you have every right to assume."

Her pulse kicked. She laid her hands over his arms and moved into his embrace. "Jake."

For the first time since she'd gotten there, his lips curled into a smile. "I'm sweaty. I smell like my backyard and I need a shower."

She smiled back. "I'm not fussy, Jake, and I don't mind getting dirty. Just kiss me."

He did, dragging her against him and taking her mouth, parting her lips and sliding his tongue inside to claim hers. His lips were salty, and she devoured his flavor, needing to consume him, to take him as much as he was taking her. She whimpered against his mouth and he lifted her into his arms without breaking the contact of their kiss.

And since his mouth was attached to her mouth, how he could maneuver his way down the hall and into the bedroom without being able to see was beyond her ability to understand. Okay, she really didn't care. All she knew was that in record time she was on his bed and they were both naked and Jake's hands were roaming gloriously all over her body, and she had free rein to explore his. Which she did in depth, kissing his mouth, his neck—as salty as his lips, before lifting her head and rolling over on top of him.

He arched a brow in a wicked, suggestive way as she rubbed against him. He was hard and positioned in just the perfect spot to send hot shivers all over her. Never one to take the initiative in bed before, Lucy nevertheless felt emboldened tonight. She pushed off his chest and sat up, rolling down a bit so she sat on his thighs. She held out her hand and fortunately, Jake knew just what she asked for. He reached over to his nightstand and pulled a condom packet from the box and handed it to her.

She tore the packet open and took the condom out, then swept her gaze up to his, wanting to watch his face as she applied the condom. The heat in his gaze, the way his eyes met hers instead of focusing on what her hands were doing, excited her more than the feel of his hot, hard shaft in her hands. When she had the condom applied, she held him in her hands and paused, riveted on the dark sexy look in his eyes.

"You gonna do something with that or just hold on to it all night?"

She grinned. "I don't know. I might."

She could tell he was fighting to maintain control. "You might what? Do something or...nothing?"

She cupped the sac underneath him and gave it a gentle squeeze. "Oh I definitely don't plan on doing...nothing."

He groaned and lifted his hips. "Lucy," he said, his husky tone a warning.

Figuring she'd tormented them both enough, she

shifted, fitting him inside her and leaning over him, pressing her palms down on his shoulders, her breasts flattened against his chest as she drew close to his face. "You have absolutely no sense of humor."

He grabbed her hips and lifted her up, then down, making her whimper. "Not when this is what I want."

Her own humor fled. Her concentration on how Jake made her feel, how his body connected to hers so intimately made her tighten around him, made her want to surge forward and grip his shoulders. She shuddered, holding that position until she thought she'd burst from the sensations spiraling through her core.

Jake swept her hair back and cupped the back of her neck to bring her lips to his, kissing her with a deep passion that stoked the fires higher than she thought possible. She was hot, wet, aching, needing release. She ground against him, controlling their passion, rocking hard until Jake groaned against her lips. He dug his fingers into her hips and started sliding her back and forth—faster, controlling her movements. She lifted her head and looked down at him. His eyes had darkened, shadowed under his half-closed lids. He looked fierce, yet so sexy he made her belly tumble, and her sex twitched in spasms she could no longer hold back.

"Jake." His name fell in a whisper from her lips as she shuddered around him, falling into a climax that tore from her body in a rush of sensation. She tensed, gripping Jake's arms and pressing her thighs to him.

Jake held tight to her hips, arching upward with one

hard, driving thrust, then pulled her in for a kiss, groaning as he released. She held him, feeling the sensations of his release, absorbing it like a hot caress. He wrapped his arms around her and held her close long after both of them had settled.

She liked being on top of him, resting against him like this. She liked it so much her lids grew heavy, especially since he stroked her back with slow, easy caresses.

She yawned.

"Are you going to sleep there tonight?" he asked.

She smiled against his chest. "I might."

"I'm sweaty."

"And now so am I."

"You know what that means, don't you?"

She lifted, placing her forearms on his chest so she could peer down at him. "That we're both sweaty now?"

He tapped her butt cheek. "No. It means we both need to take a shower."

"That smacks of promise."

"You're like a ravenous beast I can never satisfy."

She waggled her brows. "I know."

She got up and they went into the shower, which turned out to be just as much fun as she thought it would be. They dried off and had dinner together. Jake opened a bottle of wine and they spent a couple hours sitting outside in the backyard swing.

"I realized something tonight," she said, laying her head on his shoulder.

"Yeah, what's that?"

"We fought, made up, and we're still together."

"Is that unusual?"

"In my world? Yes."

He laughed and slung his arm around her shoulder. "Babe. If we're going to have a relationship, get used to it. We'll have arguments while we're getting used to each other. We come from different backgrounds. Plus, I'm kind of new at this. I haven't really had a steady girlfriend before. I'm sure I'll screw this up more than once."

Girlfriend. She was his girlfriend. She felt giddy at the prospect. It was childish, but she loved it. She loved him. Everything was new and exciting and she felt much younger than her age. Ridiculous, but she didn't care.

She was having the time of her life, in love with a very special man.

She wasn't going to let anything screw this up.

Chapter Eleven

Jake sat back at his desk and grinned, trying to concentrate on the mounds of paperwork littering his desk.

He was going to have to stop this mooning or his employees were really going to give him a hard time. Though they'd already done that. The guys had been torturing Jake for the past two weeks, claiming he smiled too much and he was—God forbid—turning into a nice guy. They said it was so unlike him they kept asking if he was sick, possibly dying.

Bunch of smartasses.

He couldn't help it. Being with Lucy put him in a good mood. And for the first time in his life, he was genuinely content. He had a great career that satisfied him during the day, and a wonderful woman to spend his nights with.

They'd been together every night, having dinner, going to movies or just hanging out at his place. Lucy would bring her laptop and paperwork with her. They'd sit side by side at his kitchen table while he worked on plans and she did legal briefs. Quiet, relaxing, homey. It was weird as hell, but he liked having her there, and she seemed to enjoy being there with him, even if neither of them said a word for hours. They'd settle into a companionable silence until one or both of them would look up and they'd make eye contact. They'd put their work away and have a beer or a glass of wine, sit outside if the weather was nice or in the living room if it was cold outside.

It was so different having someone to talk to about his day. Lucy listened well, didn't offer advice, just listened while he talked out his problems. She'd ask him what he planned to do to work out the issues. Then she'd wait until he asked for her advice instead of inserting her opinion. And she told him about her day, about the cases she could discuss or problems at the office, and asked for his advice. She treated him as an intellectual equal, listening to what he had to say.

Even arguing with her about current events and issues was fun.

After they were talked out, they'd head into the bedroom—if they made it that far—and spend a couple hours exploring each other, learning each other's bodies, their likes and dislikes. They'd already discovered they didn't have a lot of dislikes, which made Jake really happy.

Everything about Lucy made Jake really happy.

He was in love with her. He wanted her in his house every night. He wanted to share his life with her, wanted to cook with her, do his paperwork at night alongside her, and have her in his bed every night. He wanted to wake up feeling her warm body nestled against his.

He already couldn't imagine his life without her, and he was pretty sure she felt the same way, though neither of them had said "those words" yet. He wondered if she'd move in with him if he asked. He knew he lived pretty far outside the city, but they could commute together. Even if she had to work late, he could always catch up on paperwork at the trailer while he waited for her. He liked the idea of driving to and from work with her. More time together.

He was even starting to imagine the future. Converting the other bedrooms into rooms for kids. Kids he and Lucy would have together.

He'd never gone that far in his thinking about a woman. With Lucy, the thoughts were starting to come pretty easy. And frequently.

He dragged his fingers through his hair and shook his head. God, he really was pathetic, wasn't he? But hey, he was happy. Nothing wrong with that.

He straightened when Bob pulled open the door and stepped inside, a grim expression on his face.

"You aren't going to like this," Bob said, filling the trailer doorway with his bulky form.

"What am I not going to like?"

Bob tossed a stack of papers on Jake's desk. "Our permits have been pulled. The project is halted as of right now."

Jake's heart slammed against his ribs. "What?"

"OSHA is demanding an immediate inspection, claiming anonymous complaints about potentially dangerous safety hazards. The architect's plans are being called into question—something about measurements being off spec, and our building materials have somehow suddenly come up subpar and will need to be reinspected."

Jake stood and snatched the papers off his desk, scanning them all one by one. Safety, engineering and materials. All at one time. His gaze shot to Bob. "This stinks of sabotage."

"No shit."

"But who? There's plenty of work to go around. Every single contractor in the city is scrambling to find enough workers to fill their jobs. It's not like any one of our competitors would want to shut us down. People in our business just don't do that."

Bob pulled off his hat and scratched his head. "Beats me. It's not like the folks in our business resort to this level. I've never seen anything like it. You'd have to know people in all the right places to do a shutdown of this magnitude."

People in all the right places. Jake didn't make enemies in his business. He was a fair contractor who always handled his business above board. He treated his employees fairly and always brought in his jobs on time and on budget. He got along well with the other contractors, too. So who would want to ruin him, to shut his business down, to make him look like a fool?

There was only one person he could think of who hated him enough, and who had the power and muscle to do all that had been done to him.

Raymond Fairchild.

"I'll be back." He grabbed his jacket off the back of his chair.

"Where are you going?" Bob asked.

"To put an end to this."

"You know who's behind this?"

He slipped his jacket on. "Oh yeah. I definitely know who's behind this. I'll have it fixed by this afternoon. Send the guys home with a full day's pay. They'll be back on the jobsite by tomorrow morning."

He threw open the door to the trailer and stormed down the steps. He could take the truck over to the Fairchild law firm, but he figured he should walk, let the cool air calm him down.

Because right now he didn't want to talk to Raymond Fairchild.

He wanted to kill him. And if he killed the old man, he'd never get his business back up and running again.

Lucy tried her best to concentrate on strategy with her father, when all she really wanted to do was blurt out that she was in love with Jake, and her father had better get used to the idea of having Jake in her life because the two of them were going to be together.

But over the past couple weeks things between Lucy and her father had been strangely...silent. Nice, almost. Her father had to know where she'd been spending her nights, and he hadn't complained, hadn't tried to insinuate his opinion on the matter, hadn't said or done anything, as a matter of fact. Maybe he was finally resolved to the situation. Lucy was calmed by the peace between them, so she was afraid to rock the boat.

Yes, she was a coward. Besides, she really didn't know what her situation was with Jake. It was too new, too...private. They were enjoying their time together. It was blissful and perfect and she wasn't ready to share that with anyone. Not even if it meant telling her father that from now on he'd have to butt out of her personal life.

Besides, she figured he'd probably already gotten the idea that her relationship with Jake was off limits, so why beat a dead horse? If things continued on as they had been between her and Jake, and maybe in the future, if they decided to move in together...

The idea gave her chills of excitement. Living with Jake. She'd really like that. A lot. It was a step toward her future, a future that included Jake in her life. She couldn't imagine one without him now. The past couple weeks had been so incredible. Just being with him calmed her and thrilled her at the same time.

She loved him so much her heart ached.

"Lucille. Are you paying attention?"

No, she hadn't been. Not at all. She'd been thinking about Jake. The thought made her smile. "Sorry, Father. What were you saying?"

"I said on the Macarthur versus Langton Industries

case, I think we should bring in a couple of the new associates. Let them get their feet wet."

She nodded. "Good idea. I suggest Keller and Chen. They're both extremely bright and would handle the details well."

"I'll let you decide on that one. Now on Sanderson versus Idea Technologies—"

The sound of shouting outside the boardroom interrupted her father. Lucy quirked a brow. "What's that?"

"I don't know." Her father stood and turned just as the door to the boardroom was thrown open. Jake stalked in, his hands curled into fists, a murderous expression on his face. He pointed to her father.

"You!"

Lucy stood and hurried to insinuate herself between Jake and her father. "Jake, what's wrong?"

He spared her only a brief glance before skirting around her and heading toward her father. "Get out of my way, Lucy. I need to have a conversation with your dad."

Lucy's secretary, Maggie, and several of the employees craned their heads through the doorway. Mortified, Lucy shooed them out and shut the door, whispering for them to get back to work. It was embarrassing enough that they'd seen this much. She turned back toward the room. "Jake, what's going on?"

He whirled on her. "Your father is what's going on. He pulled the permits on my project."

"What?" Lucy turned to her father.

Her father held his hands in the air. "I have no idea what he's talking about. You are out of line, Mr. Dalton."

"Don't pretend you don't know what I'm talking about." Jake advanced and her father backed up until he hit the wall. "You are the only one I know who has the muscle to plant fake safety violations, faulty building materials and shoddy engineering specs."

Could it be true? Her gaze shifted from Jake to her father. "Did you do this?"

Her father went pale. "Of course not. I'd never—"

"Bullshit!" Jake slammed his fist against the wall right next to her father.

"Now see here." Her father made a move toward Jake.

"No, you see here." Jake's voice was filled with fury as he grabbed a handful of her father's shirt and pushed him back against the wall. "Quit lying to cover your ass, Fairchild. I want my permits restored by the end of the day, and I want you to stop interfering in my business. It's bad enough you stick your nose into my personal life, but if you try to ruin me I will lay you flat."

Sweat poured down her father's face, and his paleness turned pure white.

Not good.

"Jake, stop. My father's not well..."

Jake, still pinning her father with a forearm across his chest, shot her a glare. "And you're even worse than he is, automatically taking his side. You're so blind to your daddy's every fault you can't see him for what he really is—a lying, manipulative bastard who'd do anything to keep you shackled to his side."

"Lucille," her father croaked, reaching for his chest.

Oh, no. Couldn't Jake see what was happening? "Jake. Stop this now." Lucy moved toward them. "Father."

"Oh, that's just great," Jake said. "I knew when it came down to it you'd take his side."

Panic filled her as her father began to slump. "Jake, let him go. I mean it. He's hurting."

Jake pushed away from her father and, with disgust, turned around. "I don't know why I even bothered."

Lucy reached her father just as he fell to the floor.

"Lucille, please. The pain. Oh, God...it's my...heart. It's...really...my heart...this time. Get...help."

He could barely speak as he sucked in great big gulps of air in between words. She heard the panic in his voice and it ratcheted up her own. Her father was breathing fast. Too damn fast. Lucy dropped to the floor and grabbed her father's wrist. His pulse was so fast, so erratic. Oh, God.

"Maggie!" she screamed.

Her secretary flew through the door.

"Call 9-1-1 now!" she ordered.

Maggie's stricken look said everything. She nodded and grabbed the phone.

Lucy cradled her father's head in her lap, loosened his tie and unbuttoned the top button of his shirt. It didn't slow down his rapid breathing at all. "Relax, Father. Take slow, even breaths. We'll have an ambulance here shortly."

She shot a look to Jake. "You. Get out of here. Now."

Jake looked down at her with a frown. "He's faking it, Lucy."

Dear God, the man was certifiable. Anger mixed with panic, making her feel lightheaded and dizzy and nearly ready to lose it. She tried to keep her voice even, for her father's sake. "Get out or I'll have security escort you out. My father is having a heart attack, can't you see? Even I would know if he was faking."

But Jake just stood there, looking down at her, then at her father. His frown changed then.

"Lucy, I...I need you to understand what happened here."

She couldn't hold back the tears any longer, even though she wanted to appear strong for her father. "I mean it, Jake. I don't want you around my father. Or me. Get out of here."

"Let me help."

"Get out now!"

He turned and left the room without another word. Her heart broken, she sucked in a shaky breath and turned back to her father, stroking his sweat soaked brow.

"The ambulance is out front and the paramedics are on their way up in the elevators, Lucy," Maggie said.

She nodded, focusing all her attention on her father. "It's okay, Daddy." She kept her voice low and soothing. "I'm here. I'll take care of you now."

Jake stood outside the entrance to the building and watched them cart Raymond Fairchild out on a stretcher. An IV tube was hooked up and an oxygen mask covered his face. He saw EKG leads on his chest, and the concerned looks on the faces of the paramedics as they hurried him into the ambulance.

He also couldn't miss the stricken look on Lucy's face as she followed them out the door.

Jake stepped back into the shadows, letting the gathering crowd swallow him up so Lucy couldn't see him.

What had he done? Had he let his anger send the old man into a heart attack? Jake didn't like Fairchild, hated what he'd done to his company, but he'd never forgive himself for causing harm to the guy.

He walked back to the construction trailer and closed the door, laying his head in his hands.

He wasn't a violent man. But he'd completely lost it in the boardroom with Lucy's father. He'd let his anger overrule his common sense. He could have gone about this a completely different way, but instead he'd busted in and attacked a defenseless old man.

Now he'd have to answer for that.

And the look on Lucy's face...

He'd lost her. And probably his company, too.

He couldn't think about that right now.

First thing he had to do was pray that Raymond Fairchild survived the heart attack.

Chapter Twelve

Lucy sat at her father's bedside, holding his hand while he slept.

His hair was mussed. Her father was always impeccably groomed, and his hair was a mess, sticking up everywhere. She reached up and smoothed it.

At least he had some color in his cheeks now. The doctor had no results yet, said they'd need to run more tests. But her father was resting, and that was good. They didn't even have him in the cardiac unit, since the tests they'd run in the ER indicated he was in no imminent danger. So they'd brought him to the general floor in a private room, which made her stress level reduce considerably. Now all they had to do was await the test results.

He was still alive, and for that she was incredibly grateful. They might butt heads every day, but she loved her father. The thought of losing him...

He was all she had. Her only family. The only one who loved her.

Besides Jake.

Jake. She let her chin drop to her chest.

She wouldn't think about him. Not now. Not yet.

"Are you sleeping?"

Her head snapped up at the sound of her father's voice. "No, not at all." She smiled. "How are you feeling?"

"A little tired, but much better." He squeezed her hand.

"I'm so glad."

"Thank you for being here, and for...defending me. I didn't want you to think I'd ever do something so heinous."

She patted his hand. "I believe you."

"I don't want to lose you, Lucille. I need you."

Were those tears in her father's eyes? He was blinking so rapidly she couldn't tell. Overcome by guilt at how she'd treated her father the past couple months, she knew she was going to stand by his side no matter what. "I'm here for you. I'm not going anywhere."

"Thank you. It's just you and me, you know, just like it always has been."

She managed a grin. "Yes. The fearsome twosome. But you have to rest and get well so we can spread fear into the hearts of other law firms again."

He laughed. "I'll do my best."

They chatted for a bit, then Lucy said she was going to the cafeteria for something to eat, demanding her father get some rest. "The doctor said he'd be in with test results in a little while. I'll be back before then."

"I'm going to be just fine, Lucille."

She nodded and gave him a bright smile. "I know you will, Daddy."

She headed down to the cafeteria, but when she got in line realized she'd left her purse in the closet in her father's room. Rolling her eyes at her stupidity, she took the elevator back up to the floor, then hoping not to awaken her father, tiptoed toward his room. She stopped just short of the doorway when she heard laughter and low voices.

"You're a much better actor than anyone gives you credit for, Ray."

Lucy frowned. That was Alex's voice. She pressed her back against the outside wall and listened.

"Believe me, it's no easy feat feigning a heart attack. And being poked and prodded and stuck with needles was no picnic, either. But all worth it in the long run."

"Having Lucy's boyfriend storm in and throw you against the wall was perfect," Alex said.

"Yes. And all I had to do was breathe in and out rapidly. Made me hyperventilate until I almost passed out. Lucille fell for it."

"Will you press charges against Jake for assault?"

"Oh I don't know. I think putting a halt to his construction project was more than enough. And with Lucille bound to my side for the foreseeable future, I think we've driven the stake in quite deeply enough, don't you think?"

"It's never enough, Ray," Alex said with a smug laugh.

"It's only a matter of time now. Lucille will come to see the benefit of sticking with me, and eventually she'll see you're the bright spot in her future. Be patient."

Lucy put her hand to her rapidly pounding heart. She wanted to sink to the floor in frustration and utter rage.

She'd been used! Jake had been right all along. About everything. About her father, about the construction permits. Her father had used her, had used Jake.

Dear God, the man was a monster. All these years she had stood by him, hoping that somehow he would see her...that he would love her. That somehow he would wake up and be the father she had always wanted, had always needed.

It would never happen. She had made a critical mistake.

He didn't love her. Her father didn't love her. No man who loved his child would do this.

She was shaking so hard she almost couldn't remain upright. She wanted to run, down the hall, down the elevator and out the door, not face this. Never face him again.

But she couldn't. She was a Fairchild. The thought made her shudder, but she couldn't hide from who she was.

The frightened child craving love was pushed aside, replaced instead by the angry woman who didn't need anything from the man inside that room.

She had to pull it together. Fury gave her focus for what she had to do. Taking in a shuddering breath, she shored up her strength and pivoted, stepping into the room with a smile plastered on her face.

"Oh, Lucille. I didn't expect you back so soon," her father said, making sure his voice sounded weak and pathetic.

"I'm sure you didn't, Father." She nodded to Alex. "Alex."

"Lucy. I just came by to—"

"Celebrate?" she finished for him. At her father's shocked look, she said, "Oh, I heard everything you and Alex said, Father, so don't bother playing the innocent cardiac patient any longer."

She turned to Alex. "I would sooner marry a monkey than marry you, Alex. Your touch makes my skin crawl. Don't ever darken my door with your presence again." With a tilt of her head, she said, "Get out of my sight before I start screaming."

Alex made a hasty exit and she turned her attention on her father. "As for you. Today, I'm embarrassed to call myself a Fairchild. You are mean, manipulative and a vicious bastard, Raymond. No, I will never call you Father again, because the term is an endearment and I've lost all heart for you. To treat Jake, and to treat me, like pieces on a chessboard that you can move at your own pleasure, is vile and despicable. You are lower than the scum in the gutters.

"I love, Jake. I know you don't understand that

because the word love is foreign to you. I don't deserve him, because he's better than me. Better than us. You'll never get that. But now, thanks to you, and thanks to my blind stupidity, I've lost him. The only man I ever loved. And I can't even really blame you for that, because it's my fault."

"Lucille, I—"

"Do not ever speak to me again. You are no longer my father. Or my business partner. I'll send someone for my things at the house. I will not live with you, and I will not work with you. I do not in any way wish to be associated with a man who is so utterly heartless. You make me sick."

She went to the closet, grabbed her purse, and walked out, ignoring the stricken, pale look on her father's face, along with the tears she was sure had been manufactured for her benefit.

Fake. It was all fake. The man didn't have a genuine emotion to spare for her. He never had. He never would. That realization hurt much more than she ever thought it could.

She had spent her entire life doing everything she could to earn his love, his attention. And for what? So he could manipulate her, treat her like a commodity?

Her eyes were open now.

Had she hurt him by what she'd said, by walking out on him? She doubted it. Maybe irritated him because his scheme didn't work and he hadn't won. And that made her sad. Why had her father turned out this way, so devoid of emotion, of caring?

Not her problem. She shouldn't care. He would reap what he sowed, and she would feel no pity for him. She'd sided with him for far too long, bought into his manipulations, and it had cost her everything.

Everything that had been so important to her.

Including the man she loved.

Jake was hoping he wouldn't run into Lucy when he came up to Raymond Fairchild's room. He wasn't going there to see her, anyway. He was going to see Raymond. And he wasn't going to beg for leniency. He didn't deserve it. Not after what he'd done.

But he did need to face what he'd done head on, and offer an apology.

Though he wouldn't be surprised if Lucy's father didn't throw him out on the spot. Or have him arrested for assault. In fact, he was surprised that hadn't already happened, considering Fairchild's connections.

The floor was quiet as he walked toward the room. He paused, listening for the sounds of conversation. There weren't any. It was late afternoon so he figured maybe Lucy was seeing to things at the office. He peeked around the corner. Raymond was in there by himself, so he stepped in.

Fairchild's eyebrows raised, but he didn't look angry.

"Mr. Dalton."

"Mr. Fairchild."

He looked good. Had color in his face, and there were no IVs hooked into him or any other machines. That was a good sign.

Lucy's father laced his fingers together and laid them in his lap. "Have you come to gloat?"

What did he mean by that? For putting him in the hospital? "No, sir. I came to apologize. I let my temper get the better of me and I went off on you. I'm sorry. I should never have done that. I didn't mean to hurt you."

"You didn't hurt me."

"Sir, I think I did. You're in the hospital."

"Not for long. Just waiting for my discharge papers."

Jake tried to mask his relief. "You're going to be okay, then?"

"You've won, Jake. I've already made calls to release the permits. You'll be back in business tomorrow."

"It *was* you." Jake didn't know whether to be relieved or furious. Probably both.

"Yes, of course it was me. And my daughter knows everything. She overheard me talking to Alex. Celebrating. I faked my heart attack. And now I've lost my daughter. She's left me."

Jake waited to see the remorse on Raymond Fairchild's face. The hurt at what he'd caused.

It didn't appear. Instead, the man was angry.

He hated losing.

Unfreakingbelievable.

"I hope you're happy," Fairchild said.

Jake shook his head. "I'm not happy at all. I wish things could be different. For Lucy. I've never seen a woman more devoted to her father, and a man so completely blind to what he had. She loved you. And all she wanted was your love in return."

"I do love her."

Jake snorted. "You don't even know what it means."

"I've given her everything."

"Except what she really needed from you. For someone who's supposed to be so smart, you're really stupid, Fairchild."

Raymond lifted his chin and sniffed. "She's angry right now, but Lucille will come around to my way of thinking. Eventually."

"You think so?"

"Of course. She's a Fairchild. She has grown up with the finest things life has to offer. Do you think she'll be satisfied with someone like you?"

Jake let his lips curl. "Maybe. Maybe not. But I'll bet she won't be fooled by a prick like you ever again."

Fairchild's lips set in a thin line, his face turning a bright red. "You can leave my room. I don't ever want to see you again."

"Gladly."

Jake turned and walked out the door.

He thought he'd be happy to hear that his permits would be released.

Instead, only one thought occupied his mind. The

only thing that really mattered.

Lucy.

Lucy waited until the staff had cleared out for the day before she headed into the office to grab some important files. She didn't know where she was going to go after that. Not to her home. She didn't have a home anymore. And certainly not to Jake's. Not after what she'd done to him. He'd never want to see her again.

She palmed her stomach, the thought of everything she'd lost because of her stupid mistakes making her knot up inside.

She packed up the files she'd need over the next several days and picked up her briefcase, deciding to stop off at the coffee shop for a latte. As she passed by the construction site, her heart ached. She pushed on, determined to shut Jake out of her mind.

When a wolf whistle rang out, she stopped dead in her tracks and whirled around.

There, leaning against one of the huge yellow pieces of machinery, was Jake, his arms folded across his chest. God, he looked good in worn jeans and a white shirt. He pushed off the machinery and walked toward her.

"Hey," he said.

"Hey."

"I saw your father today."

Her eyes widened. "You did?"

"Yeah. I went to the hospital to apologize to him."

"Jake, you didn't have to—"

"Yeah, I did. I went off on him like a crazy man. That's not like me. I don't blow up and lose my temper like that. But I also don't like being manipulated. I knew your father had squashed my permits."

"Yes. He did. You were right and I didn't believe you. I'm sorry."

"No. I'm sorry, for embarrassing you at work, and for pushing your dad around."

She lifted her chin. "He deserved it."

"No he didn't. I should have called you with what I knew and let you do some investigating."

"And I should have believed in you right away. I'm through siding with my father. He's used me for the last time."

"I'm sorry, Lucy. I wish he could be different."

She shrugged. "I've come to the realization that he's incapable of loving me. That's not my fault. It's his problem."

"You're right, it is."

They stared at each other for a few minutes. Then Jake took the briefcase from her hands. "Heavy."

"I took several of my case files from the office so I can work at...well, wherever home will be for the next few days until I can figure things out."

He looked down at the briefcase in his hands, then swept his gaze back up to her.

"I liked having you work at my kitchen table next to me."

Her heart seemed to hover somewhere in the middle of her chest, fluttering like wild butterflies. "I liked that, too."

"We've both made mistakes throughout our attempts at having a relationship, Lucy."

"Yes, we have. And for the ones I made, Jake, I'm so sorry."

"I'm kind of new at this, so I screwed up. I'm impatient. I hated your father interfering, and I didn't take tender care of your heart and your feelings like I should have. That made me no better than him."

Dissolving into tears out here on a public street wouldn't be a good idea. But Jake was making her resolve difficult saying things like that. "You're nothing like my father. And I'm sorry for not standing with you against him. I know him better than anyone, know the level of deviousness he's capable of, and still I wanted to believe that he wouldn't have done something as horrible as shut your company down. But he did, and I'll never forgive him for that."

Jake put his arm around her and pulled her close to him, then moved them toward the trailer. "Oh, I don't know about that. Maybe that's how he wanted to show you he cared about you."

"Quit making excuses for him. He did it because he wants to control me."

"You're right. He's a bastard and he doesn't deserve to

have you for a daughter."

She laughed. "I don't want to talk about my father anymore."

"Okay. Let's talk about us instead."

Jake opened the trailer door for her and she stepped inside. When he closed the door and flipped on the lights, she smiled at the bouquet of roses sitting amidst the chaos of paperwork on his desk. She turned to him and smiled.

"I was going to come up to your office, but then I saw you walking by."

"They're beautiful. Thank you."

He pulled her against him, wrapping his arms around her. "I love you, Lucy Fairchild. Come live with me."

Her eyes widened. "You want me to live with you?"

"I want a lot more than that. I want a future with you. I want forever with you. But let's start there. We'll take things slow and step by step."

She grinned, sniffed. "I'd like that."

"I have to warn you, though, it'll be a big change in lifestyle for you. I'm just a plain guy. I don't have a lot of money, I can't offer you much, but I have a heart rich with love for you."

Lucy let the tears fall now, unashamed of letting Jake see the emotion she could no longer hold in. She pressed her lips to his, kissing him with all the love she had. She felt like she was going to burst.

"I love you, Jake Dalton. And I'm no longer rich,

either. I'm going to reassign all my cases, and then I'm quitting the firm and I'm going to go back to school."

He pulled up a chair and pulled Lucy onto his lap. "Is that right?"

"Yes. It's time I start living my dream."

He nibbled her neck and she shivered with delight.

"And what would that dream be, Miss Fairchild?"

"I want a house out in the suburbs with the man I love. And I want to be a kindergarten teacher."

He leaned back and smiled at her. "I think that sounds like a perfect life. I dare you to make it work."

She held out her hand. "I'll take that dare. You're on."

They shook hands, and this time she knew they were both going to win.

About the Author

Jaci Burton is a national bestselling author, published in multiple genres. Her life is spent juggling deadlines and trying to keep the characters straight in all her books. Jaci is an award-winning author, and has won the Romantic Times Bookclub Magazine's Reviewer's Choice Award. Jaci makes her home in northeast Oklahoma with her husband and more dogs than she can wrangle.

He wasn't part of her balance sheet. But one week in his bed could tip the scales.

To Do List

© 2007 Lauren Dane

Since she could pick up a pencil, Belle Taylor has used lists and charts to map out her life. When she achieves a goal, she marks it off her to do list. Simple. But now, just steps away from her corner-office, name-on-the-letterhead goal, she realizes that the life she thought she wanted may come at too high a price.

Exhausted, she retreats home for Christmas vacation to rethink her life, complete with all-new lists. What she hadn't expected is Rafe Bettencourt, her brother's best friend, the man who she thought only saw her as a pesky younger sister. But when he kisses her under the mistletoe, Belle finds herself with a whole new set of goals to balance with what she thought she always wanted.

Rafe knows Belle is trying to figure out what to do with her life. He also knows he's done loving her from afar, and he's not beneath making it as hard as possible for her to choose to return to San Francisco.

Because Rafe can make to-do lists too—and his plan is to seduce Belle back home where she belongs. At his side. And in his bed.

Warning, this title contains the following: Smokin' hot monkey love and naughty wish fulfillment, a few words you wouldn't say in your grandma's presence.

Enjoy the following excerpt from To Do List...

Belle let the heat of the alcohol settle into her, bringing a languid fluidity to her muscles. She sighed and looked at the man in bed with her.

"You're really gorgeous, you know that?"

"I like it when you've been drinking, Belle." He winked and she snorted.

"Whatever. You were going to tell me why you're suddenly interested in my bases after giving me sweaters for Christmas for the last dozen years."

He grabbed her ankle and yanked, pulling her down as he rolled on top of her. Wow, he was good.

His mouth met hers, insistent, wet and hot. It was just the two of them, no worries about someone walking into the hallway. She let go of her control and gave in, sliding her hands up his arms, over his shoulders and into his hair. Soft, so soft and cool against her skin.

Heat licked at her insides when his tongue confidently invaded her mouth. When he rolled his hips, she moved, wrapping one of her calves around his ass, opening herself to him and holding him in place.

He broke the kiss, and looked into her face. "Just making sure you're still with me. I think about your bases a lot. I have for several years now. I told myself it was stupid to give in but you taste too good to resist. You're here, I'm here and we're both adults who know and like each other."

"I'm still with you, although you're not feeling me up or anything, which if I recall correctly, is part of the bases thing, right? And how long? God, you've wanted to kiss me and…" she shivered violently when he trailed fingertips up her belly, against her bare skin under her tee shirt, "…do that? You just kept it to yourself when I've like had the dirtiest fantasies ever about you?"

He tweaked a nipple then as he appeared to have to make a lot of effort to breathe.

"Christ, Belle, I can't believe you just told me you had dirty fantasies about me." He leaned down and sucked her nipple right through her tee shirt, leaving her no alternative but to hold on and enjoy it.

"I do. I did. All the time. You have no idea how good you look. Or crap, maybe you do. Should we get under the sheets?"

He laughed, breaking free of her nipple and looking at her again. "Honey, it's killing you to muss these blankets isn't it?"

"Well, the coverlet will get wrinkled and…oh my…" She lost her ability to think when he reached between them, into the waistband of her loose cotton pants and stroked over her pussy through her panties.

"You're so wet and hot I can feel you through your panties."

"Fuck the coverlet. Let me touch you! Why do you keep moving away?" she demanded.

"First things first. No fucking tonight. I want us to be totally sober when that happens so I can take my time and make you fuck drunk instead. I will make you come though because I have to see it. I'd invite you to sleep with me tonight but I have to be up at four-thirty and you need your rest. Tomorrow night you *will* tell me all your naughty fantasies though."

She blew out an exasperated sigh. "Whatever it takes to get you to let me touch you."

He laughed and she thought he'd never looked sexier. Rolling away a moment, he pulled off his jeans and shorts while she made quick work of her clothes too. When he turned back to her he groaned.

"Belle, you're beautiful. A glorious invitation to sin right there wrapped in velvety pale skin." As he moved to touch her, they both gasped at the shock of pleasure from bare skin meeting bare skin.

His mouth touched every part of her. The spot just below her ear, the hollow of her throat, the sensitive skin just beneath her breasts, her nipples, the backs of her knees. All the while, his hands touched wherever his mouth didn't.

But he wouldn't let her do much other than receive pleasure. "No, Belle, if you touch me I won't last. Please, let me love you." A lock of hair fell over his forehead, obscuring his right eye.

She managed a shaky nod, needing him so ridiculously bad she couldn't speak. However, that was nothing compared to the way it felt when he slid down, between her thighs and shouldered them wide open.

Belle watched, fascinated by the way he drew his

tongue over the seam where thigh met body. He stopped, breathing her in and she knew somewhere in the back of her mind she should be embarrassed but all she felt was utterly turned on and wildly flattered by the possessive action.

And then his mouth was on her pussy and she fell back against the pillows with a gurgled gasp of pleasure. Over and over, his tongue flicked, licked and teased every inch of her pussy until she thought she'd explode.

Her nipples throbbed, her skin tingled, her toes pointed and still he drove her relentlessly higher. He devoured her with avarice, devastated her with the way he seemed to crave her cunt. No one had ever gone down on her like this.

Finally, he drew her clit between his lips, gently scraping his teeth over it while at the same time sliding three fingers into her gate. It was too much and she lost it, falling hard into an incredibly intense orgasm.

Printed in the United States
146068LV00001B/185/P